Freedom for Bron

N.S. Blackman

Cover illustration by
Robert Luke Newberry

Text and illustrations copyright
© N.S.Blackman
Cover illustration copyright
© Robert Luke Newberry

All Rights Reserved
Published by Dinosaur Books Ltd, London
Third edition: 2024
www.dinosaurbooks.co.uk

Conditions of sale
This book is sold subject to the condition that it shall not, by
way of trade or otherwise, be lent,
re-sold, hired out or otherwise circulated without the publisher's
prior written consent in any form of
binding or cover other than that in which it is
published and without a similar
condition including this condition being imposed on the subsequent purchaser.

The right of N.S.Blackman to be identified as the author and
illustrator of this work has been asserted by him in accordance
with the Copyright, Designs and Patents Act, 1988

ISBN 978-0-9930105-7-6
British Library Cataloguing in Publication Data
A CIP catalogue record for this book is available from the
British Library

"*A tour de force of accurate history* and epic adventure scenes. This is a really great book for
Year 5 and Year 6 children."
The School Run

"*An excellently written narrative* that really evokes the period, bringing the reader a
cast of characters to relish."
Parents-in-Touch

"The landscape of villages, farms and dangers for travellers is realistically drawn, and the mythology of the time is deftly conjured.
A rewarding read."
The School Librarian Journal

"The story is well researched and *makes it easy for pupils to engage imaginatively with the historical setting* as seen through the eyes of a child."
Books for Topics

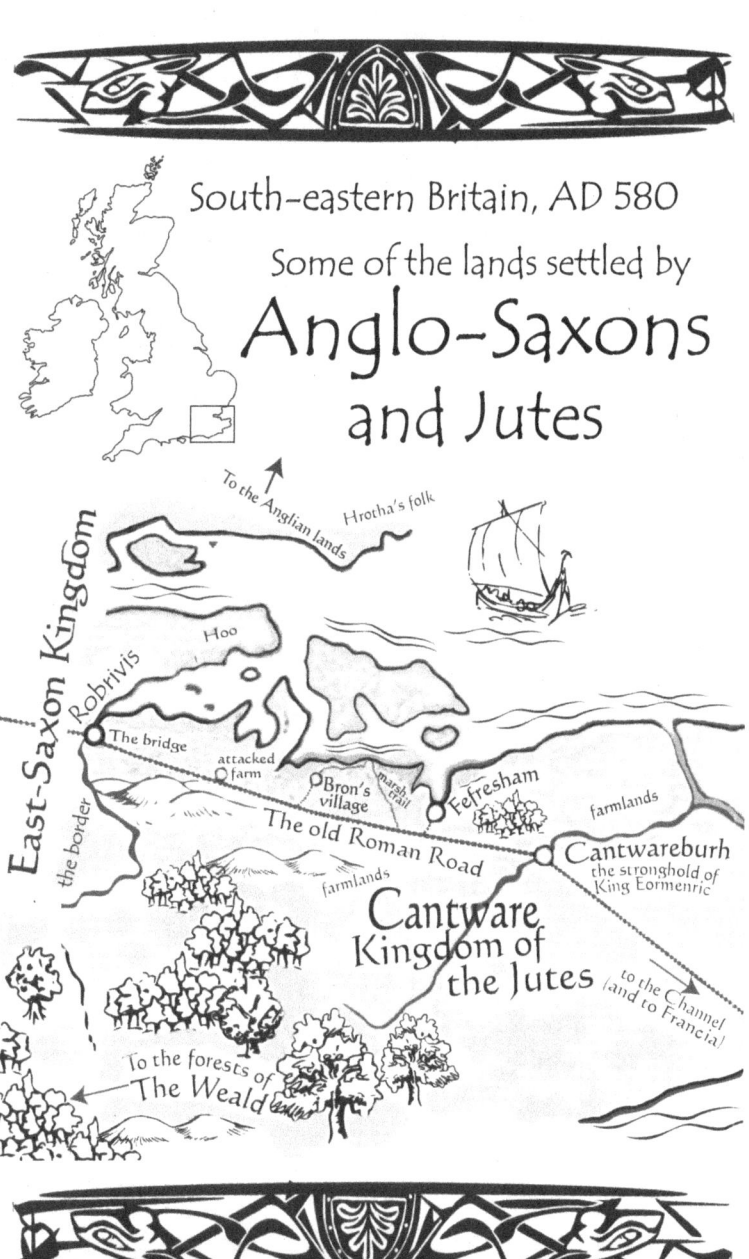

Pronouncing the names

The Saxon characters
Lord Beogard (pronounced **Bay-o-gard**)
Beogard controls his own lands, the wild Weald country. He is a Saxon and is uncle to both the the Saxon king, Bricgnytt, and the Jute king, Eormenric.

King Bricgnytt (pronounced **Brich**-nit). *He controls Robrivis, the river and lands to the west.*

Saxon warriors
Sigwyn (pronounced **Sig**-win)
Edwyn (pronounced **Ed**-win)
Kenhelm (pronounced **Ken**-elm)
Sherwyn (pronounced **Shur**-win)

The Saxon gods
Thunor (pronounced **Thoo**-nor)
Woden (pronounced **Woe**-din)

The Jute characters
King Eormenric (pronounced *Yor*-men-rik)
He controls all the land from the river to the coast

Jute warriors
Jutrad (pronounced *Joot*-rad)
Havrad (pronounced *Hav*-rad)
Fornost (pronounced *For*-nost)

Jute villagers
Bron (pronounced **Bron**)
Rowena (pronounced **Row-*ee*-na**)
Wigstan (pronounced ***Wig*-stan**)
Willa (pronounced ***Wil*-a**)
Paega (pronounced ***Pay*-ga**)
Frumold (pronounced ***Frum*-old**)

Other characters
Hrotha (pronounced **Ha-*roth*-ah**)
Cloda (pronounced ***Cloe*-dah**)
Cleava (pronounced ***Clee*-vah**)

The place names
Robrivis (pronounced **Rob-*ree*-vis**)
Frefresham (pronounced ***Fef*-ra-shum**)
Cantwareburh (pronounced ***Kant*-ware-bur**)

Prologue

The Romans ruled Britain for hundreds of years, their legions keeping order at the point of a sword.

But then the Roman Empire fell apart, and the soldiers left.

The fine stone buildings they had made fell into ruin, and their great roads became overgrown and tangled with weeds. Fear spread across the land and order fell into chaos.

New people were settling, arriving from across the sea: tribes of farmers, craftsmen, metalworkers, story-tellers, warriors, makers of gold. These tribes called themselves Angles, Saxons, and Jutes, and in time they become known as the Anglo-Saxons.

The languages they spoke would one day become English. But not yet – not for a thousand years or more. In those distant times, they still spoke in words that would sound strange and ancient to us.

At that time, they had no books, they did not read or write. The stories they told were spoken out loud, shared in gatherings beside the fire.

****

So imagine yourself beside a great fire now, warming your hands as it flames against the night.

It is winter. You are seated with your friends, your backs to the dark, your faces glowing. You are huddled in woollen cloaks, with sweet drinks of honey-mead to keep you warm, and the smell of a feast roasting. Soon you will eat.

But first... a tale!

The story begins with a group of children. And one in particular, the youngest, a boy called Bron. His eyes are keen but anxious, his knees scuffed with dirt. He is a Jute, and lives in a village of Jutes, in flat farm lands close to the sea...

****

The tale begins

The older children said they were going hunting, so Bron followed them. He hadn't eaten all day. Maybe they would catch squirrels to roast.

He went after them, doing his best to keep up.

The older ones scrambled to the top of the bank and crouched, looking down at something. Bron squeezed in behind.

That's when he saw it for the first time, the road. A wide way, cutting through the woods, dead straight and level, overhung with trees.

"The Romans made it," Olfric was telling them. "A long time ago."

Bron stared. The road stretched into the distance.

"We shouldn't stay here, it's dangerous," said Rowena. She was the eldest, and Bron always felt safer when she was around.

But Olfric carried on talking.

Bron knew Rowena was right. They shouldn't

be here – especially not him. He should be back at the forge. That's where he lived now, with the blacksmith.

But the blacksmith and his wife had left this morning at first light, without a word to Bron, without saying where they were going. They had taken the cart, its wheels squeaking as they heaved it along the track, away from the village.

Bron watched them go. His stomach had been rumbling, but he knew better than to go into their house and help himself to any of their food. His place was under a bench, beside the forge.

"Where does the road go?" one of the boys was saying.

"That way," pointed Olfric, "It goes to where the Saxons live. The other way, is to our king's hall.".

"Are the Saxons bad?"

"Dangerous. And good fighters," said Olfric, standing up. "But not as good as Jutes."

He threw a heavy stone and it thudded across the cobbles.

"One day I'll go along there. I'll go to see the king," he told them.

"We'll come," the others agreed, and Bron joined in – "we'll come!"

But Olfric looked down at him and laughed.

"You can't come Bron. You're too small. And anyway, you're a slave. Only warriors can visit the king."

Bron felt ashamed. He tried to think of something to say.

And then he felt someone pulling his hand. It was Rowena.

"We're going back now," she said. "It's not safe here."

As they headed back to the farms, she smiled down at him.

"Don't listen to them."

Bron nodded.

"Can we eat soon?" he asked.

****

Olfric never got to visit the king. A year later, a winter fever came to the village, and he was one of the children who died.

Bron grew though. He spent his days working at the blacksmith's forge. And sometimes he thought about the road, and he dreamed of where it might lead.

Summer turned to winter, and winter turned to spring.

And ten years passed…

Chapter One

A decision on the road

Beogard cursed and sat down. After a day of walking his leg was stiff and he was getting tired. He shielded his eyes and watched the three Saxon warriors racing up the road towards him.

They were running easily, keeping their spears low.

The hot sun didn't bother them.

Ten summers ago he would have moved like that and he would have been faster than any of them. Five summers even.

But not now.

These days he had to stop and pretend to

adjust his shield strap while really he was catching his breath. And his young companions had to pretend not to notice.

Beogard could tell, even from here, that they'd found something.

Edwyn reached him first and his eyes were bright. Aged sixteen, he was carrying a full length sword for the first time.

"Well?" asked Beogard.

"River-men," replied the young warrior, kneeling down next to him. "Five of them, like you said."

Beogard nodded.

"Aye lad, I thought as much. They'll have a boat hidden down there somewhere. A coward's escape on the tide and they'll be back up the coast before nightfall."

He shook his head.

Since that morning they had been following the river-men's trail, away from the burning farm. The farm, a cluster of low thatched buildings, had been a nice place before the raiders found it.

Beogard gripped his axe at the memory.

The farmer had been lying dead, still holding onto the stick that he'd tried to use as a weapon. His sword, if he had one, had been somewhere out of reach. There was no sign of the farmer's family but a dog lay panting beside him. Alive but only just. Its fur was matted and bloody.

The dog had growled feebly until Beogard laid a gentle hand on its head, talking and soothing it, before swiftly breaking its neck.

****

Edwyn was speaking again.

"Lord Beogard? Lord, we can attack the river-men now, while they're resting. We can make them pay for what they did."

"Do they have prisoners?"

"None that I saw."

"What about dogs?"

"None, lord. And no look-outs either. They don't expect to be caught."

The old warrior fell silent and watched the two others approach.

Sigwyn was a bold lass and Beogard liked her. She was fair-haired like her brother, and tall. She carried her own spear. And a sword hung from her belt. It was a fine weapon, given to her by her uncle, King Bricgnytt of the East Saxons.

Beside her came Kenhelm. Tall, young like both of the others, fast and strong.

"There's another farm down there," Kenhelm panted, his eyes glinting. "The raiders are hiding, watching it."

"Like wolves," snorted Sigwyn.

Beogard nodded.

"And there are *five* you say?"

"Yes. Or maybe six."

Maybe six.

Beogard looked at his young companions.

"That's too many. We can't fight them."

At once Sigwyn protested.

"But the farm! If we hurry we'll be able to help…"

"Six is too many. I promised the king, your *uncle*, that I'd keep you safe. I'll not risk breaking my oath to go scrapping with bandits."

"But Lord Beogard, there may be children down there!"

Her eyes flashed and she looked to the other two, appealing for support. Her brother nodded.

Beogard rubbed at his stiff knee and cursed.

Children. Of course there would be children, there always were.

"Lord?"

They were all waiting, looking at him.

Beogard sighed.

"Very well," he said at last. "Go on then. Show me this farm."

Chapter Two

Thunor, God of Thunder

Little Willa was sitting up on the farmhouse roof, waiting for the robin. Where was it? The tiny bird with its pretty song often landed up here. But now it was hiding.

The air felt very hot and still.

Willa lay down and waited. Robin would come soon.

She rested her chin on the thatch. It was warm and she could see beetles scrambling through the brown straws in front of her. If she squinted her eyes they looked like strange creatures in a tangled forest.

Magic creatures. Or wolves maybe. Willa didn't like wolves. She had never seen one, but she knew they lived in the woods. Her big brother had told her stories about them and said she should keep a look-out.

In the distance, there was a rumble of thunder. *Thunor the storm god was waking…*

Another rumble. And some instinct made Willa look behind her, back towards the hazel trees where the chickens liked scratching at the ground.

Her heart lurched with fear. A group of strange men was walking straight towards the farm.

Their clothes looked funny; they were not Jutes. And they had weapons.

Willa let herself slide down the thatch, ignoring the scratches to her face and ran straight to the work-shed where her mum and her aunts were busy weaving.

"Willa? What is it?"

"Mummy! Strangers…"

Her mum was on her feet before Willa could

finish – and her hand went to her side where the knife hung from her belt.

"Get the men," she hissed. "Run."

****

Hrotha strode towards the work-shed, smiling broadly. The river gods were being good to him today.

At the first farm, the one they'd raided earlier that morning, his sons had seized tools, silver and some quality cloth.

Hrotha had not been troubled by killing the farmer. The fool had tried to fight him with a stick. The farmer's two brats had run off crying until his own son, Hartha, had chased them down and killed them too. It pleased Hrotha that the lad was not squeamish.

"Clean your blade," Hrotha had ordered him. "You'll leave an offering at Woden's shrine tonight to pay for the killings."

"Yes father."

Hrotha smiled. Yes, the gods would be

satisfied.

And now, just as they were approaching their boat, here was a second Jute farm!

His shrewd eyes took in every detail. The menfolk were all away, working in nearby fields he guessed.

But that left the women and children unprotected.

They looked strong and healthy – good for slaves. They could be put to work on his own land or sold for silver.

A woman was standing in front of the hut now, her knife in her hand, sheltering others behind.

Hrotha strode towards her.

****

"Bring us food," ordered Hrotha. "What do you have?"

The woman stood in front of him, her eyes hard but fearful.

"Do it now! I am hungry!"

Hrotha raised his fist.

"We have meat," the woman said quickly. "We

have ale… good things. Sit for a while. Rest. But afterwards leave us in peace."

Hrotha laughed.

"Feed us. Then we'll see. What's your name?"

"I am Rowena, wife of Wigstan."

"And where is Wigstan now? Is he far…"

But before he could say another word a clap of thunder broke across the sky and shook the very ground.

Hens ran squawking and birds scattered up from the trees. Rain began to fall in thick, heavy drops.

And then, Thunor himself, the storm god, came striding out of the forest.

****

Old Beogard looked as much like a Saxon god as could be imagined. Though past his fiftieth year he was still broad and powerful.

His thick beard was streaked with grey and beneath his iron war-helm his hair was plaited at the sides and fell in waves across his mail-clad shoulders.

His arms were thick-set and burly from years of cutting timber and he held his great axe in his right hand as if it was no heavier than a willow stick.

There was another roll of thunder and he looked up at the sky and laughed.

He was dripping with water, every inch of him from head to foot, as if he had stepped straight out of the storm clouds.

Hrotha backed away and reached for the sword at his belt – all his men were doing the same.

But the giant warrior seemed not to notice them.

Instead he strode straight past and held his great arms out to Rowena.

"My niece! Ah but it is good to see you again!" he bellowed and lifted her, laughing – then he leaned in close and whispered. "Peace. Fear not. I will deal with these men for you."

He turned and knelt – still not looking at Hrotha or his men – and spoke to little Willa.

"You have grown big and strong," he said her. "Will you take your old Uncle's war axe and look after it for him?"

Willa, nodded wide-eyed, and took the gnarled ash handle which he offered to her.

The steel axe-head itself, which would be far too heavy, he let rest on the ground.

The rain was easing off again, as suddenly as it had come.

"If you can find me some cloth I'll be able to dry the edge," he smiled at her. "We must keep it sharp."

******

Behind them, Hrotha had finally recovered from his surprise and seemed to make a decision.

He stepped forwards, towards the old warrior's back, quietly drawing his sword.

Chapter Three

Dragon-Flame

Hidden among the trees behind the farm, the three young Saxons were watching all this. They saw Beogard talking to Willa. And they saw Hrotha moving towards the old man, sword in hand.

Sigwyn lifted her spear and tensed.

But Kenhelm held her back.

"Lord Beogard told us not to follow."

"We can't leave him to face them alone," she hissed.

"No, but…"

"Sister," whispered Edwyn. "Look – I think he knows what he's…"

Sigwyn hesitated, still gripping her spear.

How could the old warrior face the raiders by himself?

******

Beogard turned suddenly and seated himself on the bench beside the farmer's hut. Still he pretended not to notice Hrotha. He leaned back, spreading his legs, and the planks creaked under his great weight.

"You are wondering how I got here first?" he said to Rowena, speaking loudly so that all would hear. "You are expecting to see all my sons and my brothers too?"

He chuckled.

"Don't worry, they are coming. They'll soon be here. As you know, they are all strong men and half my age, but I raced them and I beat them."

He glanced towards the trees.

"They'll be here soon enough, crashing about like boars, roaring and shouting. And they'll be very annoyed to find me already with you."

He wiped his nose on his sleeve.

"I won the race though, fair and square. So I'll collect a silver coin from each of them."

Little Willa was staring at him, wide-eyed.

"But how could you win? How is an old man faster?"

"Ah, but I'm not…"

Beogard tapped the side of his nose.

"I tricked them, see. Those fine young kinsmen of mine are running like fools for the bridge up yonder," he pointed, "I let them go – and I swum across the river instead."

He let out a bellow of laughter and it was such a hearty sound that Willa laughed – and so did one of the young women standing behind Rowena.

"Yes, I swum. Can you imagine it? Me with all my heavy gear! It is a good job that I am so fat and float well. But I am no fool," continued Beogard.

He was suddenly serious.

"My most precious treasure I held above my head. Dragon-Flame demands respect."

And he leaned forwards, pulled back his

dripping wet cloak and revealed his sword – sliding it half from its fur-lined sheath.

It was the most impressive weapon any of them had ever seen.

The bright metal shone, gold and steel. The hilt was decorated with precious stones and the blade laced with patterns of flame. Its edges were deadly sharp.

And it was completely dry.

"It's beautiful," said Willa.

"Yes little one," chuckled Beogard. "This is Dragon-Flame, the sword of the great Hengist himself, given to me by my father Beorgwulf. For I am a warrior of mighty Hengist's line, a Lord descended from famous kings and conquerors!"

And then he turned.

And finally – now that he was ready at last – he looked directly at Hrotha and fixed him with a stare.

"And who are *you*?" he asked.

Chapter Four

Bron

Up among the trees, the three young warriors held their breath. They saw Beogard get up and stand directly in front of the raiders, one against six.

He was bigger than every one of them by a hand's length, but outnumbered.

Sigwyn could stand it no longer.

"I'm going down there."

"No! He made us promise to wait," hissed her brother, holding her back.

Kenhelm was about to speak too – but just at that moment, a farm boy appeared on the path behind them.

****

The boy was dark haired like Kenhelm, but long-limbed and scrawny. He was younger than all three of them – maybe by a year – and dressed in rough cloth, without weapons except for a plain seax knife.

A heavy bundle of sticks was tied and balanced across his shoulders.

He stopped suddenly, sensing that something was wrong.

Looking through the trees towards the farm he saw the strangers with their weapons, and Rowena and her family huddled together.

Then he turned and noticed the three young Saxon warriors staring at him.

He dropped the sticks and ran.

****

Bron sprinted up the hill, weaving through the trees.

His first thought was to get away from the raiders. His second was to reach a weapon and to sound the alarm.

His master had a steel sword that he always

kept propped beside the door of his forge. It was never used except as a sign of the metal worker's trade.

Bron would use it now, although he'd been forbidden ever to touch it.

Enslaved or not, he would run to help Rowena. And his master could call for the village men to come running from the fields.

Bron sprinted hard, but then a heavy blow landed on his back and knocked the breath out of him. He stumbled and fell. And before he could rise again a weight fell on him, forcing him to the ground.

Bron fought by instinct. He lashed out with his fist and tried to scramble free. But an instant later he felt the sharp edge of a knife at his throat.

"Do not move boy."

He made a grab at the knife. Anger gave him strength. But the blade pressed harder, cutting his neck.

"Keep still now or believe me I'll kill you."

He looked up at his attacker – up at the Saxon warrior who had out-run him – and saw that it was a girl. She was only slightly older than himself, dressed in mail, with a richly decorated cloak and a fine war-helm. The armour gave her weight, which pushed down on him.

He felt a stab of shame.

Her two friends had run up beside her and were looking down at him as well.

"Look at his rags. He's just a slave, not one of the raiders," said the dark haired one.

"He's no warrior," agreed the fair haired one.

"Those men back there are not warriors, they're cowards," replied the girl. She flipped up her knife and pushed it in front of Bron's face.

"And what about you? Are you a coward too?"

Bron felt himself blush.

"I am no coward. I was running for my sword."

She laughed.

"Slaves do not carry swords."

He glared at her.

"Neither do girls."

Chapter Five

The storm passes

Beogard stroked his grey beard and laughed, but he kept his eyes fixed and unblinking on Hrotha.

"So, you were invited to my family's feast too? I did not realise it."

Hrotha laughed.

"We like a feast but we were just leaving."

"Already? Before my sons arrive?"

"Yes. We must catch the tide."

Behind Hrotha, Beogard noticed the other men relax – a stir, a breathing out – their leader had decided not to fight.

"Then go," he shrugged. "I'll not stop you."

The old warrior took a step back but his hand still gripped his sword.

"I am only sorry that we did not meet earlier today."

If Hrotha understood the threat he pretended not to notice it.

He nodded: "Next time then."

And he turned and walked ahead of his men towards the trees.

"Come!"

They followed, disappearing towards the great river.

Beogard watched them go. He stood very still and kept listening – until at last the silence was broken by little Willa.

"But uncle! Where are all your sons?" she said. "They're really slow aren't they?"

Beogard turned at last and laughed.

"My sons? Ah, little one, they're not coming today, I was just playing a trick."

Suddenly his shoulders slumped. He looked tired and bedraggled. The brief summer storm had passed and he was no longer the god

Thunor.

"Help me get out of these wet clothes," he grunted. "Before I catch a fever."

****

Soon men came running from the fields and a crowd gathered at the farm. They began to point at the three young strangers – Sigwyn, Edwyn and Kenhelm, who had rushed out from the trees as soon the raiders had left. The farmers glanced suspiciously at the three friends' swords and their Saxon-style clothing.

Wigstan, Rowena's husband, arrived looking pale and angry. He was still holding the scythe he'd been using to cut hay.

A stocky, short-haired man came beside him, the village elder-man, Paega.

"Who are these strangers?" Paega demanded, pointing towards the three young Saxons. They now stood with their shields raised, as the villagers began to surround them.

"Saxons," said Wigstan, embracing his wife. "Did they hurt you? If so they will pay for it!"

"No! Leave them," exclaimed Rowena. "These Saxons protected us. They chased off the raiders…"

"It was uncle Thunor! He saved us!" called out little Willa. "He did it with his famous sword!"

And she pointed to the farmhouse where Beogard was sitting, his great bulk wrapped in a woollen blanket.

Paega and Wigstan looked, noticing the fine warrior's gear laid out on the ground at Beogard's feet: the gold belt buckle, the ornate sword hilt, the decorated war helm and shield.

"Lord, if you have helped my wife, then I am grateful to you," said Wigstan

Beogard shrugged.

"No worries lad."

There was a moment's silence and the farmers looked at each other. Wigstan cleared his throat.

"Well then… will you eat with us?"

"I'm hungry, I'll not deny it," replied Beogard. "And thirsty too."

"Then you must feast with us tonight," said Paega. "You and your followers."

The farmers' spears were lowered.

Sigwyn, Edwyn and Kenhelm put down their shields and now Jute children crowded round, keen to see their strange Saxon clothes and fine weapons.

At the edge of the group one figure stood unnoticed, as usual. Bron wiped at the bloody scratch on his neck. The Saxon warriors had forgotten all about him now.

He turned to go. It was time for him to return to his master's forge with his bundle of wood. He'd have to collect them all together again where they lay scattered on the ground.

Chapter Six

A feast at the farm

All work in the fields was abandoned. Tools were stacked, gates were shut and animals tethered. A fire was laid in the pit in front of Rowena's farmhouse.

Elder-man Paega and his wife brought a pig to roast, enough to feed all the families from the nearby farms. And everyone gathered, sitting on the ground and on benches, while cups and bowls were laid on a trestle board.

Wigstan and a group of the older men went to look for the raiders. Paega rode ahead on a pony and a couple of the men took swords but most went with spears or just farm tools. They soon returned.

There was no sign of Hrotha or his gang.

By now the air smelled sweet with roasting pig and wood smoke. Ale cups were passed around and Paega brought out a decorated drinking horn. Children were chewing on warm bread and some of them began singing.

"You've good land here," said Beogard. "But you should keep better watch. You're too close to the sea."

Now the men sat around, their eyes bright. They were keen to hear him. In the light from the fire Beogard's war-helm shimmered and on it the golden beasts and dragons seemed to dance in flames.

"We do keep watch," said Wigstan, shaking his head. "But this month we're all busy with harvest. This is not when trouble usually comes."

"Trouble can come any time."

Paega snorted.

"These cursed men from the river – do they not have crops of their own to gather?"

"Yes elder-man. But they'd rather steal yours,"

said Beogard. "And it's not grain they wanted. I think they were looking for plunder. And for slaves."

Rowena passed him the drinking horn, now full.

"We owe you our lives, lord."

Beogard smiled and raised the horn.

"No lass, you owe us nothing. This feast is all a weary traveller could want."

"But where are you travelling to?" asked one of the farmers. "And what are you Saxons doing in the land of the Jutes?"

Others around the fire murmured and nodded.

Beogard took a long drink and wiped his mouth on his sleeve.

"Some of us here are Saxons, it's true. And some of us are Jutes. Some may also be British folk whose families lived in this land long before us. But tonight we are all friends beside the same fire.

"To tell you the truth, I've travelled around so much that sometimes I can't remember what I am – " he laughed and put his great hands on his knees.

"But why I am here you ask? I've come a long way and it is a strange tale. I can tell it to you if you want…"

A murmur of excitement went around the fire.

"Yes, tell us," said Paega. "We want to hear."

"Very well."

A harp was produced and passed around until Edwyn took it and began playing a Saxon tune that all the Jutes knew too.

Everyone looked at Beogard, waiting for him to begin.

Nobody noticed an extra figure squeeze in at the back of the crowd.

Bron had slipped away from the forge where his master, the blacksmith, now lay snoring. Tomorrow he would have a slave's work to do again. But tonight he would listen to warriors' tales.

Chapter Seven

The visitor to the hill

Bron wrapped his arms around his knees and waited.

Beogard stood. And instantly, from his very first words – deep, slow, almost chanting – Bron was spellbound. He had never seen such a fantastic figure.

With sparks and smoke rising around him, the great warrior looked like giant, dark against the sky. He placed his hand on his sword-hilt and began.

"I am Beogard, heir of Hengist and Lord of the Weald. My hall lies in the wild forests of the south, and a year ago – *a year this very night* – I almost died in my bed.

"I would have died, there as I slept, but for one thing. I was suddenly woken in the dead of night by a sound that chilled my blood: a howling and yammering as if from a great hound. The sound woke me and I lay sweating in the dark with my eyes wide and the hair rising on my scalp.

"I am an old man and not much frightens me these days. But that dog's howl did.

"I found my courage, took up my sword and led my warriors to the door of my hall.

"They all crowded behind me as I pushed the oak aside, just the merest crack, and peered outside. And there it was! A huge grey hound, staring straight at me.

"I looked back at it. Our eyes met, and then the strangest thing happened.

"Before I could take another step a sudden wind blew up and shook the trees all about my hall. I knew at that moment that it was the god Woden himself riding through the sky, leading his hunt.

"The storm raged around us until one of the trees snapped and a great branch fell through my roof. It landed on the very spot where my bed was, and smashed it to pieces – just like this – "

Beogard snatched up a stick from the fire and snapped it suddenly in two, making everyone jump.

"We stood there terrified, clutching each other. Then the storm passed as quickly as it had come, and the dog stopped howling. It took one last look at me and trotted off into the forest."

Beogard took a swig of beer from the horn and wiped his beard.

"And I understood. The creature had been sent to warn me. If I'd been asleep in my bed I would have surely been killed."

The children stared at him wide-eyed and the farmers nodded at each other approvingly. The tale had begun well.

****

"The very next morning," the warrior continued, "I looked for the hound. But there was no sign of it. Not even a paw mark in the earth. I spent whole the day with my folk repairing my roof and mending my bed. And I kept glancing at the forest, hoping to see the beast. But I did not see it.

"I didn't see it again until exactly one week later."

"You mean the hound returned?!" exclaimed Paega.

"Aye, elder-man it came back. And in a moment I will show the creature to you – here at this very fireside!"

Now everyone stared at him amazed. Bron glanced over his shoulder towards the surrounding trees and the younger children huddled closer together.

"Fear not," laughed Beogard. "The hound saved my life, remember? It was sent by the gods to help me not harm me."

He took another drink and continued his tale.

"This is how it happened. Exactly a week after Woden's storm another visitor arrived at my hall, a mighty warrior in a fur cloak.

"'I come from the East Saxons,' he said. 'Sent by King Bricgnytt to find Beogard, Lord of the Weald.' 'You're in luck then lad,' I replied. 'I am Beogard, the keeper of Dragon-Flame, the sword of Hengist.' And I lifted this very sword to show him, slipping it just a little from its sheath. Seeing this, he bowed and asked if we might speak together. He told me that his name was Sherwyn and that he had an urgent message. 'I'll hear your message gladly Sherwyn,' I said. 'But first we'll drink.' And I asked my daughter to bring out two cups of sweet honey-mead."

Now Beogard leaned forward, and whispered in loud voice to the children.

"It's very nice for me to taste mead in the morning as my daughter does not usually allow it."

"Why not?" called out Willa.

"For no good reason," replied Beogard. "Except that she is bossy."

The children laughed. More wood was brought and laid on the fire.

The old warrior stood and continued his tale.

And now it seemed to Bron as if he was actually there, in the far away feasting hall, on the high hill, watching the two men talk.

"The messenger drank his honey-mead and he licked his lips. And I did too.

"I eyed him, wondering what King Bricgnytt's message to me was – I had fought beside the king's father many years ago but Bricgnytt himself I had not seen since he was a lad.

"I soon had my answer. The messenger cleared his throat, put his hand on my shoulder and told me what he had come to say. King Bricgnytt wanted to meet me. He wanted me to visit him at his stronghold at Robrivis.

"As soon as Sherwyn told me this I laughed. 'Why should I make such a journey? Can't you see how old I am? I have no wish to leave my home and go roaming the country.' But I could see that the messenger was troubled.

"He lowered his voice and spoke now so that no one else could hear. 'I'm afraid war is gathering Lord Beogard,' he whispered. 'A war such as we have never seen. A great battle is coming between the Saxons and the Jutes and many good folk will die. But you might help. With your famous sword Dragon-Flame you might find a way to keep the peace…' 'Me?' I asked. 'What can *I* do?'

"'Men will listen to you,' he replied. 'Even kings. Come and speak to Bricgnytt.'

"And suddenly my heart missed a beat. For *that* is when I saw the hound again, at that very moment. Because Sherwyn leaned forward and handed me a gift: a golden brooch from his king – this one here…"

Beogard pointed to the rich ornament clasped to his cloak.

Bron watched as the warrior unpinned it and tossed it across to the other side of the fire, to where the children were sitting open-mouthed, listening to his every word.

"Pass it among you," he said. "Look at the creature shown in the gold. See its shining eyes? Its flashing teeth? Well that is the very same hound – the one that I saw in the night outside my hall!"

The children gasped. Bron leaned forward,

trying to catch sight of the brooch for himself. He managed to glimpse the gold, a dog's head encrusted with jewels, and then it was passed on.

The old warrior pulled his cloak around himself and shivered.

"So now I had to think hard. This treasure was a sign from the gods, I was sure of it. The hound was warning me again. It was commanding me to leave my safe hall and make the journey to the king."

Chapter Eight

The king's bridge

"So I left my hall and travelled with Sherwyn. And on the way we were met by Sherwyn's son Kenhelm –" Beogard paused and pointed to the young man sitting beside him. The boy nodded, stern faced.

"This is Kenhelm, son of Sherwyn, a fine young warrior. His only fault is that he doesn't much like Jutes – but I think that is changing. Now that he has finally tasted your ale he starts to love you a bit more."

Everyone laughed and Kenhelm blushed.

"And the same is true of brave Sigwyn here and her brother Edwyn. I met them on the journey too. They are of the East Saxons, yes, but I think they are ready to call you Jutes their friends.

"But their uncle, King Bricgnytt – well, *that* is a different matter.

****

"I met King Bricgnytt at his stronghold, Robrivis. Have you been there? No? It is a fine town by the river, with a stone wall all around it built by the old Romans.

"When I arrived King Bricgnytt bowed, treating me with honour, for his father and I were kin.

"'Come Lord,' he said. 'I have something to show you. We are re-building our great bridge.'

"And then he took me to see the ruined bridge which once spanned the river. When I was just a boy this bridge used to stretch from bank to bank – until one night when Woden smashed it with a storm.

"But now I saw that men were climbing all over it, fixing new beams. 'Now my men will come quickly in time of war,' said Bricgnytt. 'If the Jutes ever attack Robrivis, my warriors will race across this bridge into their land.'

"I nodded and stroked by beard. 'But what will King Eormenric and his Jutes think?' I asked him. 'Won't they suspect that you are planning to *invade* their land.'

"Bricgnytt shook his head. 'But if you will help us mighty Beogard, Lord of the Weald, if all your folk will join us, if the Sword of Hengist will fight on our side, King Eormenric will never dare to threaten us.'

"So now I understood. King Bricgnytt wanted to get my folk on his side. 'We must defend our land from the Jutes,' he protested. 'Will you not help, uncle?'

"This was a difficult situation and I had to think carefully. I did not want to offend Bricgnytt. But nor did I want to make an enemy of Eormenric.

"I wondered what to do – and then I remembered the sign from the gods. The hound was speaking to me, I thought, warning me to do something.

"So I replied at last, with the only answer I could think to give: 'I *will* help you. And your people. I'll go to see King Eormenric myself. I will tell him that you want peace and that your bridge is not a threat. And then the two of you can meet and sort out your arguments by talking. You both have enough enemies raiding along the river without fighting between you.'

"And he agreed – reluctantly."

Beogard stood silent for a moment, and looked at the farming families gathered around the fire.

"You spoke right," nodded Paega solemnly. "We do have enough enemies along this river."

Others around the fire nodded, agreeing with the elder-man.

"So now you know why I am here," replied Beogard. "And you know where I am going with these Saxon friends."

"May the gods bring you luck," said Rowena, drawing Willa close to her.

"You will need it," added Paega. "For our King Eormenric is already making plans for war. His messenger may come to us any day. And when his command comes I will have no choice but to answer. I will have to lead these good farmers to fight for him."

He looked at Beogard and his face was grim.

"I do not want to. We have no wish to leave our homes, to kill Saxons or be killed by them."

Beogard nodded.

"And you are right. There is no good in war, elder-man, only sorrow. But take heart, there is still time to stop it. I will speak to King Eormenric and do my best to change his heart."

Huddled at the back, Bron was listening intently as the great Lord spoke. But his eyes strayed often towards the three young warriors, sitting at his side in their fine armour.

He saw Sigwyn staring into the flames, then glancing at her two friends. They were on their way to meet the fearsome King of the Jutes. Were they afraid, Bron wondered? They did not show it.

Then, more food was passed around and the story telling continued until the fire died.

Chapter Nine

Standing watch

The wood burned low until only the glowing embers remained.

The talking ended and, one by one, the families left and went back to their farms. At first light they would rise again to work in their fields.

Bron slipped away too.

He followed the path through the trees – the path where he carried wood each day, stacking it to make charcoal – and reached the clearing where the blacksmith's home stood dark and silent.

But he didn't go to his bed.

The forge was in front of him, the covered pit where Bron spent his days heating iron and helping to hammer it into shape.

And beside it was the thatched store shed where he had slept every night since he was a child, on a bed of straw matting.

But tonight he couldn't sleep. He was wide awake – so he turned away, and walked back along the path. He was thinking about the great bridge at Robrivis and trying to imagine what it must look like – *a bridge strong enough to carry an army.*

And he was thinking about the Saxon warriors who were not much older than him, but who were so much better.

They wore fine clothes, they had rich weapons, they were free to leave their homes and travel.

And more than that, they had each other as comrades – sworn friends for life against all enemies. Bron remembered the way they had stood together, shields locked, when the farmers had surrounded them. And he'd seen their determined looks when the name of King Eormenric was mentioned. If war did begin, those three friends would face it together.

They weren't like him. They didn't sleep alone in an old store hut.

"Standing guard lad?"

The voice came out of nowhere. Bron spun round and saw a bulky figure looming out of the dark. It was Beogard.

"Lucky I didn't mistake you for a raider –" he raised his hand and Bron saw a glint of silver, a knife. "You can't be too careful out here."

"I…I was walking. I couldn't sleep…"

"Same here. Too much pig in your belly I expect. That's what keeps me awake – although you look as if you need a good meal more than I do. You're far too skinny, if you don't mind me saying."

Bron bowed and turned to leave.

"Wait up lad, don't go on my account. You were here first, I'll leave you in peace."

The old warrior turned away, but then stopped.

"Am I right – you were the boy who fought with Sigwyn? I saw you listening at the edge of the feast."

Bron hung his head.

"It wasn't much of a fight. She knocked me down. She could have cut my throat."

"Well don't feel too bad, she's a trained warrior. And from what I hear, you didn't have a weapon."

"No. I was running to get my master's sword," Bron began to explain – but then he shook his head bitterly. "Not that they believed it. They thought I was a coward, running to save my own skin."

Beogard nodded.

"It's bad to be seen running away lad, I won't pretend otherwise."

He scratched the back of his head.

"You know, you could always use a stick if you have to, I mean if you have to fight without a weapon. I was in a battle once and my sword was – well, it was lost – so I just grabbed a bit of wood and clobbered the man who wanted to kill me." He grinned. "I remember how disappointed he looked…"

Bron managed to smile.

"Take heart lad," continued Beogard. "*You*

know that you're not a coward – and the gods know too. Don't worry what men say. Or women. Be true to Woden and be true to yourself. When the day of battle comes that is where you will find courage – not in fine garments or famous weapons…"

Bron was amazed. No great lord had ever spoken to him like this before, as if he mattered, as if he could be worth something.

"Thank you lord…Lord Beogard…"

The old warrior shrugged.

"That's my bit of wisdom lad. For what it's worth. One thing is certain. If war does come we'll all need to ask the gods for courage…"

Then he fell silent for a while, looking out towards the river where the moon was now rising above a fine mist. Suddenly he turned to Bron.

"Here. I want you to have this."

He reached back and lifted something over his head – a cord with a woven disk tied to it.

"A warrior should always carry a lucky charm. Take this amulet. Who knows, maybe it will help you get your freedom one day."

Bron took the necklace, astonished.

"I...I thank you lord!"

"Guard it well lad, it comes from the gods and it will bring you luck."

He put a friendly hand on Bron's shoulder.

"And now I'll be gone and leave you to your watch. Stay alert and be ready. I must rise early tomorrow. I have a king to talk some sense into..."

The old warrior turned and ambled away into the shadows.

And he was smiling to himself.

Of course he'd known all along that the lad wasn't a coward. Sigwyn had told him that. When Bron was down, she'd said, she'd seen defiance in his eyes, not fear.

Chapter Ten

The war party

The next day at dawn, while Bron still lay sleeping, a line of Jute horsemen came riding along the old Roman road. There were more than twenty of them, heavily armed and riding hard. They drew up not far from the village.

Their leader, Jutrad, raised his hand for silence. He looked down at the ground. The grass glistened with summer dew but some of the taller stalks had been broken, pressed down.

People have walked here…

Jutrad dropped lightly to the ground to look more closely.

He was gathering fighters, leading them to King Eormenric's stronghold at Cantwareburh. But something else was on his mind too. Yesterday a farm had been attacked – a farmer and his children killed – and a group of Saxons had been spotted on the road.

Saxons. Jutrad was determined to find them.

He was a lean man, sharp-eyed and humourless. There was a deep scar behind his ear. It ran down his neck and beneath his mail coat onto his shoulder. Some young fool had got drunk and argued with him at the king's feast last year. The boy had paid with his life. But Jutrad's own wound had taken many months to heal and it was still painful.

"What do you think Havrad? Were these tracks made by the Saxon dogs?"

He nodded towards a forest path that led away from the road.

"Hard to say, lord. There are many farms down that way, near the marshes."

"Farmers will be busy in their fields, not out on the road," Jutrad replied. "No – I say others have been here."

He turned to the troop leader behind.

"Romulf, wait here with the men."

"Yes lord."

"Havrad, you come with me. Let's see if the Saxons are hiding down here…"

Jutrad kicked his horse on again, onto the woodland track.

****

Beogard woke early and rolled out of the bed that had been made up for him in the weaving shed.

He found that Rowena already had the fire lit again with a stew bubbling over it.

"No lady, we've eaten enough of your food already," he said. "We'll be on our way."

"I don't care how much you eat," she replied. "If you hadn't come to us when you did…"

She shook her head.

Beogard smiled.

"Don't thank me, it was our young Saxon friends who made me come here."

Just then Sigwyn appeared, walking back from

the nearby stream with a pot of water. Willa was next to her, carrying a small pot of her own.

"Sigwyn says I can be a warrior like her," the little one called out.

Beogard laughed.

"Good! And you will be a fierce sword-sister!"

But then he turned and spoke quietly to Rowena again.

"If war comes, it could reach you here soon. Maybe in a few days. I am afraid of what might happen. More dangerous men than a few river-raiders may find you…"

He looked over his shoulder, towards the trees, and it was as if he could already hear the beat of horses approaching.

"Be ready Rowena. When the time comes, act quickly. If you don't feel safe here by the water, my country is a good place. It is wild and rough – but you and Wigstan could make a home there. Bring all your folk."

Rowena leaned forward and embraced him.

"Just travel for a week. Six days to the west and another south," he continued. "Ask for me by name."

"You are a good man," said Rowena. "My mother told me that only farmers are truly good, that warriors just live to rob and kill. But she was wrong."

"Maybe," he replied. "It depends on the warrior."

And then he looked up – Wigstan had appeared. The farmer had a spear in hand.

"Lord Beogard, I have an idea…"

****

The woodland path narrowed and Jutrad kicked his horse forwards. He ducked his head beneath a low hanging branch.

He felt certain that he was on the right path. Suddenly Havrad called out to him.

"Look lord! Here."

"What is it?"

Jutrad turned his horse and rode back.

There was a clearing beside the path where more grass had been trampled down, Jutrad had seen that. But Havrad had found something else too.

The earth had been softened by rain yesterday, and close to a tree where somebody had sat there was a clear dimpled pattern in the mud.

It was unmistakable, to a warrior's eye at least. The mark of a mail shirt!

"I was right…!"

Jutrad drew his sword and kicked his horse on.

A short way further he reached a farm – a cluster of low buildings in a clearing. A child – a girl – was helping a woman to clear cups and bowls from beside a smouldering fire. The little one looked up at the riders. She ran to the woman afraid – but the woman straightened, seeing that the horsemen were Jutish warriors.

Jutrad called to her.

"Is your husband with you?"

"Nearby," she replied, her hand resting on her seax knife.

Jutrad smiled and the scar on the side of his face twisted.

"We mean you no harm. But you should be watchful. Raiders attacked a farm further west."

"We know of it," she answered. "Our men are keeping their weapons close today."

"It was a full day to the west. How did this news reach you here?"

The woman hesitated.

"The raiders came here. I think they would have attacked us too... but we defended ourselves."

"You did well," replied Jutrad. "How many were there?"

"Six."

"Saxons?"

Rowena shook her head.

"Raiders, men from up the coast – they left on the tide."

Jutrad frowned and turned his horse around.

"And you were feasting last night I see. You had guests?"

"Our neighbours. We ate together and thanked Thunor for protecting us."

"Thunor, eh? He put in an appearance did he?"

Jutrad looked north towards the river. The woman did not like him, he could see it in her eyes. But no matter. She was only a farmer's wife.

"Your days of feasting are over woman. Tell your husband that war is coming. The East-Saxons are arming against us."

And then he kicked his horse on, back towards the trees.

"Get to your work. Get the harvest in. Your men will soon be called to fight for the king."

Rowena watched him go, holding Willa close to her side.

She breathed a sigh of relief and glanced towards the river herself. Then, she thanked the gods that Beogard and his three young Saxon friends had set off just a while earlier.

They had walked out, following a muddy trail through the marshes. Wigstan had gone as their guide. It would be safer, he'd said, to travel off the road.

"Aye, it may be so," Beogard had agreed.

And the gods had just proved him right.

None of the Saxons had noticed the lone figure of the skinny boy watching from the edge of the woods. And they could not guess the pang of sadness he felt as they left.

Chapter Eleven

The waking forge

Bron went back to the forge. As usual he was hungry. He stood for a moment listening to the dawn birds. Close by, he could hear Frumold still snoring in his hut. The blacksmith would not wake for a while, maybe not even until the sun was fully up, but when he did the first thing he'd do is check what work Bron had been doing. And he'd find some fault with it.

Whatever Bron did, it was usually wrong.

"Why isn't the fire lit boy? Shift yourself, I need it ready… Why *is* the fire lit boy? I'm not ready yet, you're wasting my charcoal…"

Bron could picture his master heaving himself

out of bed and stretching in the door of his hut, chewing on a chicken leg, then walking out of sight – off to the midden pit to relieve himself.

He did the same thing every morning.

Bron stood still for a moment longer, enjoying the peace.

He looked down at his hand – last night he had slept holding tight onto the warrior's amulet – the leather cord with the woven disc tied to it.

He gazed at it. Now, in the dawn light, he could see that it was made of blue cloth with a forked symbol on the front in gold – those were the lightning bolts of Thunor, the talisman of a warrior!

Be true to Thunor and Woden – when the day of battle comes that is where you will find courage…

Beogard's words were clear in his mind and more precious to him any he had ever heard… *even if others doubt you…*

Bron hung the amulet around his neck and made himself a promise. Whatever drudgery lay ahead of him and however much Frumold nagged and moaned, Bron would think of the warriors. He would remember them always. And he no longer felt ashamed when he remembered how easily the girl had knocked him down. She had been so skillful, he thought.

Then he began his day's work – clearing yesterday's ashes from the forge and shovelling in a new heap of charcoal. It was the first of many that he would fetch and feed into the forge to make the metal glow hot.

Chapter Twelve

The hidden path

Wigstan led the travellers through a series of low fields where cattle and sheep grazed, then they climbed up a steep bank and found themselves looking out over a vast landscape of grass, mud and water. There were clusters of wading birds as far as the eye could see, picking at the wet mud or standing in channels of water that flowed between reed covered islands. The birds paid them no attention.

Wigstan pointed east, far away across the flat marsh, to where the land rose higher.

"While the tide is out, this path is safe," he

said. "If we walk fast we'll be on high ground before the water rises."

"Let's be quick then," said Kenhelm. "I don't swim."

Sigwyn shivered. She had heard stories about evil spirits that lived in the marshes – waiting to trick unwary travellers and lead them astray into the drowning mud. Even in this bright morning light, her heart warned her that the tales must be true.

****

After they had gone for an hour, a dark shape loomed up on their left. From further back it had been hidden behind a bank of reeds, but now it came clearly into view.

The remains of a huge ship were resting in the mud. It was now just a line of wooden ribs, jutting up like bones. Rotting planks clung to them, the remains of the hull. Even in its ruin it was impressive.

"Is that a warrior's ship?" called Edwyn.

"It looks like it," replied his sister. "Maybe it's

the boat of Hengist himself."

"No," said Beogard. "When he died his ship was buried with him under a great mound with much treasure."

"This boat has been here for years though," said Wigstan. "When I was a boy it had a carved dragon's head."

He pointed to the prow but where the dragon had once been there was now just a jagged beam, jutting up against the sky.

"It was a warrior's ship then," said Sigwyn.

And she raised her spear in salute.

"Let's move," called Beogard. "The tide is turning."

****

It was almost noon when the path finally began to climb to higher ground. For the last part of the journey the water had been rising steadily around them as the sea flowed in. It began filling the mud flats on either side and lapping against the long embankment where they walked. The wading birds had gone and the lower islands were submerged.

Kenhelm, walking at the back, felt the wind pick up, and the power of the tide rising behind him.

"Not far now," called Wigstan. "The road lies ahead."

They were coming into fields again and a line of trees was in front of them.

At last they stopped and sat to eat. Beogard rubbed at his knee.

"The damp air here does not suit me," he said. "I'm happier sitting on top of my hill in the forest."

"You'll soon be away from the river," said Wigstan. "Keep following this path south and east. You will reach the road by nightfall. From there, it is a short way to Cantwareburh."

They thanked him.

"But it will be dark before the next low tide," said Edwyn. "Will you wait here alone until morning?"

Wigstan laughed.

"No. I am a local man, remember. I have

cousins nearby and I will follow the dry way home through those fields –" he pointed – "I'll be with my folk before sunset."

"And they'll be glad to see you," said Beogard. "When you get home set a watch Wigstan, you and your neighbours. Watch the water, and watch the road. Keep your weapons close."

"We will."

They rested for a while and ate together. Then it was time to bid Wigstan farewell – each in turn gripping his arm.

Beogard watched as the farmer walked away, then he turned abruptly.

"We must go quickly now. Time is short. No more resting until we reach King Eormenric."

****

Back at the forge Bron was looking at the amulet again – then suddenly he heard his name being called.

"Bron! Where in Tiu's name are you? Clear out this mess or I'll take my stick to you…"

Quickly, he hung the charm around his neck.

"OK, I'm coming."

It had been a while since Frumold really had attacked him with a stick – probably because the smith was growing older and lazier, thought Bron. Since his wife and son had died he had become ever more gloomy.

And there was no affection between Frumold and Bron.

Bron could remember his real parents, just about. They had died when he was only three summers old, or maybe four. One day they had been there, and the next they were gone.

All he had left of them was a memory of kindness – a smiling face, strong arms lifting him, calling his name – and as he grew up, in his worst days, he still dreamed about them.

Last night he'd had the dream again. But it had changed.

This time he'd felt something powerful and new: not just longing for the past but hope for the future.

In the dream he had seen Beogard and the Saxons again, coming to the farm – and how tall and fine they'd looked with their swords and armour. They had come to find him, to take him with them as a warrior.

It was only a dream but it had made Bron's heart soar. He wanted to remember it so that the feeling wouldn't end.

Take heart lad…

He tucked the amulet beneath his woollen tunic and went to work, cleaning the ashes from the forge.

Chapter Thirteen

The charm's secret

Bron worked all day, just as he always did, keeping the fire in the forge burning and fed with charcoal. Whenever Frumold shouted for him, he would step in to fan the flames until his arms ached and his skin was burning, feeding the fire with air and making the flames hotter.

He checked on the pigs and chickens and made the midday meal.

Bread and salted fish.

Frumold had tools to fix – a rusting scythe blade to patch-up, a harness-link to replace, an axe-head to sharpen. None of it was skilled work, and he did it with no pleasure.

Farmers did not ask for their tools to look good or to be decorated, and Frumold did not offer it. He hammered metal, nothing more.

And now he was sleeping, sprawled in the shade beside his hut. Snoring.

It was mid-afternoon and these days Frumold often slept at this time.

Bron wasn't allowed to rest until sunset. He was kneeling beside the forge, working to finish the scythe-blade, sharpening its edge on a sandstone.

Later today, or tomorrow some time, Olgwyrd, the farmer who owned the scythe, would come to collect it.

He would bring a coin, or some small goods to trade in payment. A length of cloth maybe, or some cheese.

Or he might send his son Lognard.

Bron didn't like the boy – Lognard was younger than Bron, barely ten summers old, but he showed no respect.

"You're just a slave," he had laughed once,

when nobody else was near to listen. "When I am grown I'll be a farmer. I might decide to buy you and make you work for me."

Bron had almost knocked him down, smashing his teeth with his fist, but he had stopped himself. Just.

Lognard had smirked and walked away.

"Back to work, slave."

****

Now, as he remembered this, Bron pushed harder and felt the stone grind into the scythe edge.

And then the amulet that he was wearing, the gift from Beogard, got in the way. The leather cord snagged between the stone and the blade edge, and it was torn in two.

Bron cursed, horrified – the precious amulet fell down into the forge ashes.

He dropped the file and scrambled to pick it up.

As he patted it clean, wiping his hand across the blue cloth with its forked-lightning symbols, he froze.

There, just visible between the weave of the cloth, was a glint of gold.

He looked more closely, turning the amulet over in his hands.

For the first time he noticed that it was folded over at the top, like a purse. And the edges were held together by… by a fine bone needle.

He pulled at the needle and the purse opened.

And then suddenly the gold ornament was glittering in the palm of his hand.

It was the brooch, the precious hound-jewel that Beogard had shown to everyone last night by the fireside.

Bron stared at it, amazed.

It must be a mistake.

The Lord of the Weald could not have meant to give him this!

But Bron's heart was beating fast, racing with excitement – he remembered Beogard's words, and he knew that it was no mistake.

It's a gift from the gods…maybe it will help you get your freedom one day…

****

Frumold sat up, coughing and scratching his head. Cursed lice…

"Boy? Bron? Where are you?"

He blinked, groggy, and saw that the sun was already below the tree tops. It was late!

"What are you thinking of? Why in the hag's name didn't you wake me you idiot? I've got work to do!"

Bron appeared then, stepping out from the store-shed.

Frumold blinked at him.

The boy was wearing his heavy cloak. His hair was braided and neatly tied back. He was carrying a bag strapped across his shoulder.

"What's that? What are you up to?"

"I'm leaving."

"The hell you are. Get over here."

Frumold was on his feet, looking around for his stick. When he found it, he lunged towards Bron, swinging it wide and fast. But the young man stepped aside, grabbed the stick and pulled it from him.

Frumold was stronger by far – his arms were knotted from a lifetime of hammer work. But he was getting slower, clumsier.

Frumold swung his fist but Bron stepped clear again and the blacksmith staggered and tripped over.

"You'll pay for this!"

"I will pay," said Bron, standing his ground. And he held up the gold ornament. "I'll pay with this. I am buying my freedom."

Frumold stared at the hound brooch.

His mouth opened but he was too astonished to speak.

Chapter Fourteen

The elder-man decides

Frumold didn't want to accept the payment but Bron stood his ground. An excited group had gathered at Paega's farm to hear the dispute.

Bron had walked there with Frumold staggering after him, cursing and shouting, and news had spread through the fields.

Now Paega said he would hear what each man had to say.

"As elder-man here I will speak for the king's law."

Frumold glared angrily at Bron.

"The law be damned Paega. You know I raised

and fed this boy from a pup. He's my slave."

"Peace Frumold! You know the law as well as I do. A slave may buy his freedom – and Bron has worked hard for you, so he has earned his keep."

Paega turned to Bron.

His face was kindly, but his expression serious.

"Bron, the price for freedom is very high. Ten silver pieces is the law. Do you have that much?"

Bron was aware of the people gathered around, watching – Wigstan, Rowena and family. He saw the look of concern on Rowena's face. She and her husband had always been kind to him.

In the hard winter three years ago, when he was starving, they had shared their stale bread with him.

"Yes. I have this," replied Bron. "I think it is enough."

He held out the hound brooch and Paega studied it, his eyebrows raised in surprise.

"This is more than enough!" he exclaimed. "But how did you come by it? It belongs to Lord

Beogard I think – he showed it to us last night."

Bron nodded.

"He gave it to me as a gift."

"Ha! That's a lie!" snorted Frumold. "Why would a great lord give this to *you*?"

Paega looked at Bron – and Bron felt himself begin to blush.

"He did give it to me! I don't know why – except that he spoke kindly to me."

Frumold laughed, disbelieving.

Paega sighed and shook his head.

"It seems strange. Perhaps if Lord Beogard returns this way we can ask him. But until then…"

"Wait!"

It was Rowena.

"I believe that Bron is speaking the truth."

Everyone turned to look at her.

"Do you know this for sure?" frowned Paega.

"I believe it. Bron tried to help us when the raiders attacked our farm yesterday. Lord Beogard spoke of it – and he said that he had given Bron a gift."

"This fine brooch?"

"I cannot say…" she hesitated. "He laughed when he told me about it and said he'd given the boy a charm for a warrior…"

"Yes!" exclaimed Bron. He held up the cloth amulet. "This is the charm – and the brooch was pinned inside it."

Paega held out his hand.

"Let me see."

Bron lifted the amulet over his head and passed it to the elder-man. Paega looked at the bone pin and saw how it opened as a purse. Everybody waited.

"The brooch was inside, yes?"

Bron nodded.

Paega slid the brooch into the amulet, seeing that it fitted perfectly.

Paega looked up.

"Bron will have his freedom."

Frumold cursed.

"And this treasure is worth thirty silver pieces at least," Paega continued. "Frumold, you will pay Bron the difference, less three pieces for his clothes and possessions."

Then the elder-man looked at Bron.

"You are a free man now," he said. "I am glad for you and may Woden's blessing go with you. But if ever it is found that you lied, then your life will be forfeit."

Bron nodded.

"I swear to Thunor that I do not lie."

"So I believe."

Then Paega embraced him, Frumold grudgingly clasped his hand, and the farmers gathered round to wish the new free man well.

******

"What will you do now, Bron? Will you marry?" asked Rowena. "Who will it be?"

Willa gave him a bowl of hot broth and he ate hungrily, wiping at the side of the bowl with a piece of bread.

The family was gathered round him and a small fire had been lit to celebrate. This was where they had met for yesterday's feast when Bron had sat at the edge, hoping not to be noticed. In just a few hours his life had changed completely.

Bron shrugged, embarrassed.

"I haven't thought about it…"

But in truth he had. All afternoon, while Frumold had slept, Bron had been running through ideas in his mind, the things he might do.

He had gathered his possessions together and used a brush to clean the dried mud from his winter cloak.

He had stared at the golden hound brooch, checking again to make sure it was real.

It was. It shone warmly in the afternoon sun, clean against his skin. It was the most beautiful thing that Bron had ever seen.

Almost.

Mid-afternoon he had gone up through the trees to the Stone of Blood, the shrine where villagers left offerings to the gods every feast day or when they were sick.

He had knelt in front of the huge, moss-covered monolith, silent in its hollow, and offered up a prayer to Woden, the chief of gods.

He had done the same thing in the past, creeping here with his heart beating when nobody was watching.

Here the power of the gods was always strongest, making the hair on his skin stand up. But this time it felt stronger still. This time it had felt as if the stone was waiting for him. And when he had prayed he seemed to hear a reply.

Be true to Thunor and Woden… and be true to yourself…

Lord Beogard's words again, echoing in his mind as if Woden himself was speaking them now.

When the day of battle comes you will find courage…

Bron had left the clearing quickly and gone to finish packing his bag.

He knew what he was going to do.

As Frumold continued snoring in the late afternoon sun, Bron had sat braiding his hair. He wanted to look like a warrior.

******

Rowena poured more broth into Bron's bowl. "Well?" she asked gently. "What will you do?"

She glanced at her husband.

"If you want, you can live here with us for a while."

Wigstan nodded his agreement.

"Yes, why not? Until you decide what to do Bron. You can help me with the harvest – and next year we'll build you a place of your own up there by the trees."

The farmer clapped him on the shoulder.

"A man with silver and his own house. Then you'll find a good wife, eh?"

Little Willa clapped her hands excitedly.

"And I can help look after the babies!"

Everyone laughed and Bron felt himself blushing.

"I think Bron has other plans," said Rowena.

Bron nodded.

"I must leave you," he said. "I have a debt to pay."

Chapter Fifteen

A meeting on the road

The king's army was gathering. Over two hundred Jute men had come together that noon at Fefresham, including many with horses. They set off towards Eormenric's stronghold at Cantwareburh. Their king was waiting.

The riders cantered along the centre of the road, their iron horse shoes clattering on the cobbles, much as the cavalry of Rome once had.

Groups of men on foot walked at the sides. Each brought his own armour – mail vests, spears, shields, swords and axes. Shields were worn strapped to their backs, and war-helms were carried in the same way. When the battle was reached, the straps would be loosened, the helmets put on, and the shields lifted. Most men, then, would be gripped by fear and start praying to the gods, but for now their spirits were high. Jutrad had reined in his horse and watched, grimly satisfied.

These warriors were the first, the strongest and the elder-men from their villages, some with their brothers and sons.

It was a good turn-out and only the start.

If it came to war, *when* it came to war, ten times this number would gather on the road – farmers, men and boys summoned from the fields. If they didn't have swords, they would come with spears or farm tools.

King Eormenric had not commanded Jutrad to summon them yet. Not while crops were being harvested.

But he may soon have no choice. The enemy's bridge at Robrivis was being rebuilt day by day. King Bricgnytt's Saxon warriors were gathering. They might not wait for harvest.

And anyway, sometimes it was best to strike first.

****

Beogard and his three young companions reached the same Roman road late in the afternoon.

They scrambled down a bank, high with grass and nettles, and suddenly it was in front of them, the same cobbled way that they'd set out on the day before. They had reached the road again.

"Take care!" warned Beogard, signalling for the others to step back.

"Why?" frowned Kenhelm. "What are you afraid of?"

"He's not afraid," corrected Sigwyn. "He's being cautious – are you not, lord?"

She looked at the old warrior but he smiled and shrugged.

"It's all right lass, there's nothing wrong with being afraid," he said. "Fear has kept me alive this long. The trick is knowing when to ignore it… "

He was staring at the road.

"Look. Many boots have trampled along here today, and the iron shoes of horses. Men are on the move…"

"Jute warriors?" asked Sigwyn.

"Aye, King Eormenric's men… but I hope not all his people. Not yet…"

He knelt to study the tracks. When he stood again they could see that he was troubled.

"If war has already started then nothing we do will stop it. And we will be in danger all the while we are in these lands."

Edwyn was standing by the edge of the road, looking west towards home. A heavy cloud, in the shape of a hammer, was crossing in front of the sun.

Thunor sky-shaker's hammer.

He stared. Somehow that shape seemed ominous, like a warning from the god…

Then some instinct made him glance back along the road — just in time.

"Men!" he hissed. "Warriors!"

"Quick, all of you!" ordered Beogard. And he led them up the bank, into the woods.

"Get down and be still!"

****

They kept low and waited. A short while passed, a tense silence grew and the young warriors felt their hearts beat harder in the stillness. Then the line of Jute fighters came into view. Bearded, most of them, and with plaited hair similar to Beogard's. They walked past just a few feet away, in twos and threes carrying spears, shields and swords.

Beogard watched them closely.

Then suddenly one of the Jutes stopped. Frowning, he looked up at the bank. The trampled grass and broken nettles were telling their story.

This way, look up here...

"What is it brother?"

Another man had stopped beside the first and now he too was staring up at tracks.

Beogard cursed under his breath.

"Thunor's teeth! Just walk away can't you..."

But now other Jutes were stopping too and swords were being drawn.

"Who watches us? Show yourselves!"

For a moment nobody moved – a crow cried above them in the branches as if laughing – then Beogard sighed.

"We are seen."

He stood – but signalled for the others not to follow.

"If they attack me don't try to help. Get clear and get yourselves home."

And before they could argue he was gone, stepping out onto the road.

****

Beogard held his arms out wide.

"Rest your weapons," he said. "I walk here as a friend."

The Jutes ignored him. Their leader stepped forward, raising his sword. "I am Fornost, elderman. Speak fast old man! Who are you? Why do you hide?"

"I am Beogard, son of Beorgwulf, kin of Hengist," he answered, seeming not to notice the steel blade in front of his face. "I am travelling."

"From where? And where do you go?"

"My hall is far to the south, four days from here in the wild hills."

Then he grinned.

"It is a rougher land than yours I will admit Fornost – plain wild some say and the soil is harder than a boar's tusk – but I will speak plainly. We make better beer than you Jutes do."

A couple of the Jutes laughed. Beogard continued.

"I travel to see your king, my nephew. I ask that you let me pass," then he raised his voice. "And if we may be friends, then one day you can come to my hall and I'll let you taste my beer. But don't all come together, lads. Some of you look a bit thirsty…"

More laughter. At last Fornost smiled too and lowered his sword.

"What is your business with our king?"

"I bring an important message from King Bricgnytt in Robrivis. It is an offer of peace. And as a sign of truth I carry this. It is Dragon-Flame," he rested his hand on the sword's hilt. "This was the blade of Hengist, my forefather, who was descended from Thunor himself. King Bricgnytt and King Eormenric are of the same line so this blade should unite them as kinsmen and allies. They have enemies enough, Fornost, without fighting each other. There are many who wish to attack these rich lands from over the water, from the north and the west."

Men crowded round to look closer at the sword. Beogard pulled it from its sheath to show the riven-flame pattern on the blade.

"I have carried this all my life. And it has served me well."

"It is a precious thing indeed. But why does such an important messenger travel alone?" asked Fornost.

"I am not alone."

Fornost stepped back and raised his sword again – but Beogard laughed.

"Peace, elder-man. It is no trick. I am here with three companions," he explained. "They are kinsfolk of Bricgnytt himself. But I commanded them to keep hidden until we knew whether you would let us pass."

"Then tell them to come out," the Jute nodded.

"I will, if you promise not to attack them. Otherwise, you must kill me first for I swore to keep them safe."

The old warrior waited.

And at last elder-man Fornost nodded.

"I believe what you say," he said. "They will not be harmed."

"My thanks," replied Beogard. "I'll not forget your kindness."

And he waved for his friends to come forward.

But even as Kenhelm, Sigwyn and Edwyn came out from among the trees a new sound reached them. The heavy beat of hooves.

Beogard and Fornost turned to see a group of horsemen cantering fast along the road towards them.

The rider in the lead was a powerful looking man with a scar running from behind his ear down the side of his face.

****

The riders halted. Beogard and the others watched as they reined in their horses a short distance away along the road.

The horses kicked at the ground, agitated – they had been riding hard and it was hot.

The lead rider, the man with the scar, leaned forward to speak to some men who were standing beside the road.

As they spoke, the horseman looked up, straight towards Beogard and his Saxon companions.

He nodded, speaking some more but not shifting his gaze.

He turned back to the riders behind him.

He was giving an order.

And then swords were being drawn.

******

Elder-man Fornost stepped forwards.

"Wait!" he called out. "These Saxons are under my protection. They come in peace to see our king."

But the riders did not seem to hear him.

They were circling, lining up, their horses' hooves pawing the ground.

"Take care Fornost," said Beogard.

"You are under my protection," said the elderman.

"They mean us harm," replied Beogard. "They'll not listen…"

The old warrior knew battle-lust when he saw it. He turned to his companions.

"Keep together and move back to the trees…"

Then he stepped forward to stand beside Fornost, freeing his shield from its strap and gripping hard onto Dragon-Flame.

He had barely drawn the sword when the riders kicked forwards, yelling and digging at their horses flanks. The Jutish warriors on the road jumped clear to let them through.

"Stop! Wait!"

Fornost stood his ground. He stepped out in front of Beogard and held up his spear. But the rider in the lead didn't stop. He kicked his grey stallion harder and it smashed into Fornost, hurling him backwards.

The elder-man lay unmoving on the road.

Beogard stepped over him, trying to protect him, grabbing the rider's leg and dragging him to the ground.

"Wait!" he bellowed. "I'm not here to fight!"

But second rider came on, swinging a sword at him. Beogard staggered backwards, blocking the steel. Before the horseman could strike again Beogard smashed his fist up into the warrior's helmet and knocked him clean from his horse.

A third man attacked, and Beogard felled him with another punch. Then a fourth rider came on, and another behind.

Now he was surrounded. The three young Saxons ran to help him, hurling their spears. But even as they did so, the fallen Jute leader scrambled onto his horse again. He kicked it forwards, now coming from behind, and thundered his sword down onto Beogard's shield. The shield splintered and the old warrior fell to the ground beneath the rearing horse.

Chapter Sixteen

To follow a warrior

Bron left the farm that evening and made his way quickly to the road. The worn cobbles were just about visible – stretching ahead – a ribbon of grey leading into the dark.

A new moon was rising over the flat land, not too bright and perfect for walking by.

This road was dangerous for any traveller alone, but less so in the dark. Bandits might be lying in wait at any time but under cover of darkness a careful person could pass by unseen. Bron's eyes were good and his ears were sharp.

He walked quickly along the Roman way, alert for any sound or movement. And he kept his spear gripped firmly in front of him.

****

The night air was cool on his face and Bron felt free and alive, more alive than he'd ever felt before. But around midnight clouds began to cover the moon and it became harder to see.

Slipping away from the road, Bron found a place to sit in the deep darkness beside an oak tree. There, wrapped in his warm cloak, he sat thinking.

What lay ahead, and where was he going?

He knew for certain that he was not far from the settlement of Fefresham beside the creek – he had travelled this same road with his master just a year ago, visiting the forges there. But now he was no longer enslaved. And that meant he must plan his own way and decide what to do for himself.

Beyond Fefresham, further east, he knew that Cantwareburh was less than a day's walk.

Cantwareburh, the king's great stronghold where his warriors feasted.

But what would Bron do when he got there?

He lay down now and pulled the cloak around himself more tightly.

He wasn't sure. Not exactly.

All he knew is that he wanted to find Lord Beogard. And he wanted to see the young Saxon warriors again. He was sure about that.

****

Bron woke at dawn and immediately felt a pair of eyes watching him. There, almost within reach, a young stoat was studying him with its hunter's gaze. Bron lay perfectly still and returned the look – unblinking like the stoat. A second later the little creature turned and darted away.

Seeing the stoat reminded Bron of Frumold. The blacksmith always cursed at wild animals that came near his forge – hurling stones at them. For that reason, Bron never did.

Now he sat up and reached for the bread that

Rowena had given him. He looked around as he ate.

He was pleased to see that he had chosen a good spot to sleep, in a sheltered clearing close to the road.

A sudden thought came to him. There was the great oak at the edge of the clearing with its wide crown. A smooth chalk stone was gripped among its roots.

Bron pushed at the stone – it moved.

He took the seax knife from his belt and dug at the earth and moss surrounding it. The stone came free to reveal a hollow space beneath.

Bron took half of his silver coins and dropped them into the hollow. He pushed the chalk back on top and pressed the moss and earth around it.

Now, whatever happened on his journey, he would be able to return here for his silver.

He just had to remember this place from the road. He looked at the tree again, fixing its shape in his mind.

Goodbye Father Oak, guard this treasure for me and I'll see you again soon…

He picked up his spear and was about to step out onto the road when he heard a sound.

He froze.

It came again – louder this time – clinking metal.

Then a figure appeared on the road, barely an arm's-length away from him: a tall Jutish warrior, bearded and with cropped hair.

The warrior walked on, not spotting Bron. But Bron stood rooted to the spot, fixed by dread.

The stranger had a sword in his hand – a fine sword with an ornamental ring on its handle.

It was Dragon-Flame, the sword of Hengist. The sword of Lord Beogard.

Chapter Seventeen

The tall Jute

Fefresham was the most important Jutish settlement west of Cantwareburh. With over a dozen large buildings lining the muddy creekside, and more dwellings beyond, it was more than just a village. Fefresham was a trading post, well sited between the estuary and the road.

Under King Eormenric's rule it had grown prosperous as a place for landing goods and for trading in metal.

Bron had been here before and he knew the smiths – there were three forges and all of them were better than Frumold's.

Last year, while Frumold had haggled irritably over the price of iron, Bron had slipped away to watch the smiths at work and admire their fine craftsmanship in gold, silver and steel.

These were the forges where King Eormenric had his weapons and armour made.

The tall warrior, the man carrying Beogard's sword, was heading there now.

Bron followed him, keeping well back on the road but matching his pace.

His mind was racing and the feeling of dread deepened.

Why did this man have the precious sword? What had happened to Lord Beogard and the three young Saxons?

****

When they reached the town Bron lost sight of the man. A boat was being loaded beside the creek and people had gathered to help lift baskets and to watch. The warrior pushed his way through the crowd and slipped from sight.

After a moment of panic Bron spotted him

again and hurried behind.

A dog sniffed at his leg and then he bumped into someone – "watch where you're going…" "sorry…" Then he stopped.

The warrior was talking to someone – a small woman with a bent back – outside a low wooden building.

Bron knelt, resting his spear, and pretended to check his shoes.

Now the woman had turned and disappeared through a low doorway into the building. The tall warrior ducked in behind her.

****

The sun climbed higher in the sky and Bron sat waiting, watching the doorway.

It felt strange to be sitting here alone, with no master to wait on or worry about. He was free, but now he felt burdened in a different way.

As he ate more of the bread he thought about the three Saxons again.

Where were they? What had happened to them? Lord Beogard would never give up his sword, not unless…

A seagull landed nearby, eyeing his bread. Bron ignored it and tried to think.

The boat at the jetty was being pushed off – its sail filling, catching the breeze.

Then suddenly the warrior appeared again, ducking out through the doorway.

But the sword was not in his hand.

The man looked around for a moment, shielding his eyes from the sun, and headed back towards the road.

Bron stood.

Should he follow the warrior or speak to the woman?

****

He made up his mind to speak to the woman. He would do it quickly, find out what he could, then hurry after the tall Jute.

Approaching the low building Bron remembered that he'd been here once before – this house belonged to Cloda, the Frankish smith. And the small woman was his sister, though Bron didn't remember her name – Cleava? Cleda? She had spoken to him once, when he'd stood entranced, watching Cloda at work. She had a strange way of speaking, being from Francia over the sea, like her brother.

But she had been kind to the young slave boy whom everybody else had been ignoring.

"You like the gold child, yes?" she had smiled.

Bron had nodded.

"It's beautiful."

"Yes my brother has great skill. This will be drinking horn. A gift for the king…"

Now, as he approached, he saw that the sister looked older than he remembered, and more stooped.

She looked up at him. And to his astonishment she smiled.

"You have grown tall I see. A young man with a spear of his own now. Ah, but you still like gold I expect?"

Chapter Eighteen

The Frankish smith

Cloda sat in silence, his sister beside him, listening as Bron told his story about Beogard and the Saxons and their urgent mission to meet King Eormenric and prevent a war.

They were in a small, inner room at the back of the hall. Cleava had ushered everyone else out – servants and other members of the household – and pulled a deep red woven cloth across the doorway.

The Frankish smith now sat, with his chin on his hand, listening. The arms of his chair were shaped like wolf heads and they were more richly carved than anything Bron had ever seen. The wolves snouts were decorated with blue-green jewels and their teeth glinted silver.

The smith himself moved no more than they did. In the semi-darkness it was hard to tell if his eyes were even open.

At last Bron finished his tale.

"I was going straight to Cantwareburh – but at dawn I saw that tall warrior with Lord Beogard's sword and I followed him here. I am… I am fearful about what it means."

Bron waited but still the smith said nothing. Then at last he turned to his sister.

"This is an interesting day," he said, his voice soft. "What do you think Cleava? We've had two visitors with strange stories to tell. Who will come next, I wonder?"

He leaned forward and lifted the corner of a cloth that was lying on the floor in front of him.

"Is this it – the sword that you speak of?"

Bron's heart skipped a beat. Dragon-Flame!

"Yes."

The smith nodded slowly.

"So. Now I will tell you what I know of it. And after that, we will decide what to do."

****

Cleava left then, slipping out past the hanging cloth. In a moment she returned with a bowl which she pressed into Bron's hands.

"Stew," she said. "Eat it and listen."

Bron accepted gratefully.

"The warrior you followed is named Havrad," began Cloda. "And he was sent here by his lord, Jutrad. Jutrad is a hard man with many battle-scars, one of King Eormenric's chief warriors."

Cloda's dark eyes fixed Bron's now, warning him to heed the words. "He is not a man to cross."

Bron nodded, feeling his pulse beat faster.

"First we will talk about this sword. Dragon-Flame you called it? Yes, well you are right I believe. This *was* the sword of Hengist. This ring here, on the hilt – see it? – this was a symbol of Hengist's house, a sign of favour from the god Thunor. And this blade –" he ran his finger along the cold steel face "– this was made with great skill. The metal was folded and beaten many times in a flame that was exactly right, not too hot, nor too cold. It was created by a sword-smith with knowledge. Few of us can make this pattern so well – it is beautiful is it not?"

Bron nodded.

"It is also strong and hard wearing. Which is why Jutrad sent it to me. I have the knowledge to work on this weapon. The handle is worn and scarred – here, see? It carries the mark of many battles. Jutrad wishes for it to look new again, and for it to become his own sword."

"He cannot take it!" exclaimed Bron. "Dragon-Flame does not belong to him!"

Cloda looked at him gravely.

"A sword such as this belongs to whoever is strong or clever enough to take it. I am afraid, Bron, that your Lord Beogard was neither…"

"What? You cannot say that!"

Bron put down the bowl and glared at Cloda. Cleava rested her hand gently on his arm.

"Peace Bron. It is not my brother's fault…"

"I…I am sorry… but Lord Beogard is a brave warrior and he gave me my freedom."

"Then I am sorry too," continued Cloda. "For Beogard and for you. He was attacked on the road yesterday. The young Saxons, the three you spoke of, they have been taken to King Eormenric to face judgement. They are accused of being raiders, of attacking a Jute farm."

Bron jumped up.

"They are not! They didn't do it! They *saved* us from the raiders!"

"Then I hope they can prove it," said Cloda gently. "For the punishment will be harsh."

"But what about Lord Beogard? Why did they not take him?"

Cloda leaned forward and lifted the corner of cloth, covering the old sword again.

"Lord Beogard was mortally wounded. He lies dying at the road side, or he may be dead already. If he was a great warrior, as you say, then Woden will welcome him into his hall."

Bron gripped his spear.

"No! I must find him. I *must* return Dragon-

Flame to him."

"Find him, yes," replied Cloda. "Look on the road to Cantwareburh and I hope you are in time."

The smith placed his hands on the wolf-carved arms of his chair and stood too.

"But I cannot let you take the sword. If this weapon is not here when Jutrad sends for it, then I will be killed – and my sister too, maybe. Would you have that?"

"No of course not," snapped Bron. He clenched his fists, fighting his frustration. "But a warrior should always die with his sword in his hand. You must understand this – even slaves know it…"

Cloda sighed.

"I am sorry. I am a skilled smith but a poor fighter, and I wish to live. I cannot help you in this."

Cleava stood and looked up at Bron and her eyes were filled with sadness.

"Go quickly. Find your lord. If he is dead, see that he is buried with honour. Bring him peace."

Chapter Nineteen

Blood on the road

Bron ran hard, leaving Fefresham in the distance and sprinting back towards the road. There was no sign of Havrad, the tall Jute, nor of Jutrad his lord.

But Bron didn't care whether anyone saw him or not.

He simply ran, determined to find Beogard.

And as he sprinted he touched the amulet at his neck, praying to Thunor.

"… remember him, help him and I will follow you all my life…"

But the god was silent and tears pricked at Bron's eyes.

A pair of crows flew up from the road ahead and he stopped.

The ground had been trampled. There were deep hoof prints cut into the earth beside the road. And something was lying there, broken.

A shield. Its leather face had been ripped from the ash planking behind and the prized metal boss was missing.

A battle... men on foot... men on horseback...

Then Bron saw something else too. A cluster of flies danced around the cobbles in front of him. Blood, thick and dried.

Warrior's blood...

And at that same moment he felt something cold press against his neck.

****

"Do not move."

The voice spoke quietly, calmly. "Tell me, did you know these people?"

Bron tried to turn and look, but the blade

pressed harder, pricking his skin.

"Answer me – did you know the Saxons?"

Bron tried to ignore the pain.

"Yes. I knew them."

"Stand and face me then."

Bron stood and turned slowly. The man in front of him was not the tall warrior Havrad, as he'd expected, but a stranger.

He was dressed simply and his sword was plain, undecorated.

He looked at Bron and there was anger in his pale blue eyes.

"My name is Harnost. My brother Fornost died here yesterday, cut down by his own people. He died because of the Saxons."

"I am sorry but…but how did it happen?"

Harnost ignored the question.

"You are a Saxon?"

"No, I am a Jute. But I wanted to help them."

"Help Saxons? Why?"

"They needed to get to Cantwareburh."

"For what purpose?"

"To see our King Eormenric."

Harnost frowned.

Bron continued.

"They did not come to harm us. They came to offer peace."

The man studied Bron, unblinking.

"Peace…"

And then he lowered his sword.

"So, it was true what they told us," he said grimly. "And my brother was right to believe them…"

He turned away.

"Follow me. Your friend is dying."

****

Elder-man Fornost had been buried beneath a beech tree.

A simple pile of stones covered his grave and two men knelt beside it, their heads bowed. Four others, lads from his village, sat nearby, talking quietly.

As his brother Harnost approached, leading Bron, they stood.

"How fares the Saxon?" asked Harnost. "A

friend has come to see him."

The young men looked at Bron.

"He bleeds no more," said one. "But he will not wake. His spirit is gone."

There, slumped against the side of a tree, was a great figure wrapped in a brown cloak. A spear lay beside him on the ground.

Bron hurried forward.

"Lord Beogard… it's me, it's Bron, the boy from the farm…"

But there was no answer.

"I found the gold brooch, and I bought my freedom… I came to repay my debt to you… I know I can never do that but at least I wanted to try…"

Silence.

Harnost now laid a hand on Bron's shoulder.

"He will soon be with the gods. He does not hear."

But even as he said it, Beogard stirred.

"…Bron?…I remember you…of course…you found it then?…"

"Yes! Yes lord! I found your golden hound!"

"…good…I am glad…"

His eyes flickered closed again.

"…no debt to pay, lad…"

And he said nothing more.

****

The day grew hot and airless.

The Jutes sat together beside their leader's grave and Bron stayed with Beogard, watching his breathing grow fainter.

Some time after noon, Bron grew tired too and his head began to nod.

And then suddenly his name was being called.

"Bron?"

It was Harnost.

"Bron, look…"

A small pony was approaching.

He blinked. The rider was dark haired and wearing a cloak that was almost black – and at first Bron did not recognise who it was.

"Where is he? Where is the fallen warrior?" demanded the rider.

It was a woman's voice – gentle, and strangely

accented – Cleava.

The blacksmith's sister climbed down and pushed through the men.

She handed something to Harnost – a clay bottle.

"Boil this in water. One cup please. Quickly."

And she looked up at Bron.

"Bring it here –"

She was pointing to the long bundle of cloth tied to the pony.

Bron ran to the horse and untied the cords holding the cloth – and he gasped. Dragon-Flame, the sword of Hengist, dropped heavily into his hands.

****

"But your brother! What will happen when Lord Jutrad comes for the sword?"

"My brother is skilled," she interrupted. "He can make a copy. In fact, he is already doing it. Now peace, and let me speak to this dying warrior…"

Cleava pulled Beogard's hands together onto

his chest, and covered them with her own.

"Enter Woden's hall now. Go as a warrior and go with honour. You have fought hard. The gods will welcome you…"

Her voice grew softer and she leaned forwards, speaking very quietly, close to him.

"But Beogard, son of Beorgwulf, I think that Thunor would have you rise again."

"Rise again?…must I?"

"Yes. If the gods wish it."

She pressed the hot cup to his lips.

"Drink this and we'll see."

He drank.

"But I am old. Tired."

"Yes. I am old too. But I have to stay up all night cooking and cleaning… and this boy Bron, he is tired. He ran all the way here to bring you something."

And she nodded to Bron.

Bron's heart was racing.

He leaned forwards, lifting Dragon-Flame.

Gently, he pressed it into Beogard's hands.

The warrior's grip tightened at once around

the weapon and his eyes flickered.

"Bless you lad…"

His breathing grew stronger.

"Good," said Cleava after a while. "Life returns. Thunor is not done with you yet."

"… not done yet… an oath to keep…"

"Then keep it, warrior. Up you come, up! And do what you must."

And, to Bron's amazement, the small woman with her thin arms heaved Beogard's great bulk forwards.

He sat, wincing, and looked around.

"Beer." he gasped. "By Woden's backside your potion tastes foul. At least get me some beer…"

Chapter Twenty

Prisoners in the stronghold

At that moment, in the centre of Cantwareburh, three prisoners were being led towards the king's hall.

Edwyn stumbled and fell. His hands were tied with leather and he landed heavily, hitting his face on the ground.

"Brother!…"

"I'm alright…"

He struggled to his knees, then stood.

The Jute warrior beside him shoved him forwards, following after Sigwyn and Kenhelm.

They halted. In front of the king's hall the three Saxons were forced to kneel and crawl into a cage made of rough wooden pales, built against the side of a stone wall.

The wall was high and made with brick – the ruins of a Roman tower – but it offered them no shelter from the weather or from the hostile stares of the townsfolk.

"There you will stay, as Lord Jutrad commands it," said their captor. "When our mighty King Eormenric arrives he will hear of your crimes and you will die."

****

The three Saxon friends sat grimly, huddled together against the wall. Hours had passed and now the townsfolk were ignoring them. Earlier on, a small crowd had gathered, keen to see the prisoners, and to goad them with insults. But now nobody was paying them any attention.

Suddenly Kenhelm sat up.

"Look," he hissed.

Two lads were walking past with a bundle of weapons in their arms.

"Those are ours! That's my sword!"

"Don't worry," said Edwyn. "We'll get them back soon enough, when the King Eormenric hears our story."

"You think so?" replied Kenhelm. "I say King Eormenric will believe his man Jutrad. I think we will die here today."

A silence settled over them, and then Sigwyn looked up.

"So then we'll die," she said. "But before they can kill us we'll speak the truth and the gods will hear it."

She held out her hand and her companions clasped it. They held to each other tightly. As they did, each felt their fear grow less – for a while at least.

Chapter Twenty One

Walking together

Cleava left Beogard and the Jutes, taking the clay medicine bottle with her but leaving the pony, despite their protests.

"You will need the horse," she said. "You, I mean –" pointing sternly at Beogard.

Beogard didn't argue. He grimaced, allowing himself to be helped onto the pony. Then the group set off along the road, with Beogard sitting awkwardly and Harnost leading the way.

After a mile the old warrior climbed down again.

"She's not looking now is she?" he grunted. "I'd rather walk."

"The horse prefers it too," grinned one of the lads.

****

Bron walked on one side of Beogard, carrying his war-helm and pack, while Harnost went on the other side, letting the old warrior lean on his shoulder.

"Your brother was a good man," said Beogard after a while. "I am sorry that we brought him trouble."

"It was not you," said Harnost. "Others carry the blood guilt."

"Still, I am sorry Harnost."

Then he looked ahead.

"I only hope we'll be in time to help those young Saxons. They were in my care."

****

They followed the road east as fast as they could, though it was not quick. Beogard was struggling. After a while one of the lads –

Harada – took the pony and rode ahead.

A while later they saw Harada again.

He had tethered the horse to a tree and got a fire going. The sweet smell of roasting meat greeted them as they approached – the carcass of a young deer lay nearby.

Harada grinned up at them.

"What took you so long?"

"Nothing. We've been sitting behind that tree," replied one of the others. "Watching you work."

Beogard looked visibly stronger as he ate.

Bron noticed the colour return to his face. A skin of ale was passed around.

And then suddenly Beogard began talking.

"I once had a battle with a neighbour," he said. "He was a very boastful man, big and full of himself. I wouldn't have minded but he was also stupid. I knew that if I didn't do something soon I would end up fighting him, just to shut him up…"

"What did you do?" asked Bron.

Beogard took another bite, chewing happily and the men waited.

"One night – after some beer that is – I

challenged the fool to a wager. I bet him five silver pieces that I could catch a bigger deer than him – with bare hands only, no bows allowed, no spears or even knives."

He wiped his hands on his trousers and chuckled.

"That man fancied himself as a good hunter. He was always going on about it, on and on…"

"And you won," said Harnost.

"Eh? Well no. Not exactly. I'll tell you as we walk," replied Beogard, heaving himself up. "Now I think we should press on to Cantwareburh. What do you say Bron, lad?"

"Aye, Lord! We should go."

Bron had never felt so happy. The warrior was talking to him like a trusted friend.

They stamped down the fire and set off again. Harada rode ahead once more.

****

"Hunting deer takes patience," continued Beogard. "Have you tried it lad?"

Bron nodded.

"Once or twice, lord. I helped elder-man Paega."

"Well then you know what I'm talking about. It's no good crashing around making a lot of noise…"

They were following the road across a wide meadow now – a landscape of tall grass and flowers and the air alive with insects. Beogard breathed deeply.

"…I like this place. It reminds me of home… look lad, beehives."

He pointed – somebody had set up three hives beneath a pair of lime trees.

The sun was low at their backs and Beogard still had not reached the end of his story, when they heard hooves on the road ahead.

Harada came galloping back into view. He reined in the pony and looked down at them.

"The stronghold is close, but now you must hurry," he said. "King Eormenric is feasting with his lords and your Saxon friends are to be taken before him."

"Let's be quick then," said Beogard.

And a sudden change came over him.

He took his war-helm from Bron and set off again much more quickly. All trace of good humour had left him and Bron marvelled at the change.

With each step Beogard began to seem more like the image of Thunor that he had first glimpsed through the trees at the farm. The warior strode ahead in silence and his face was set and grim.

The other men followed and nobody spoke.

Now Bron knew.

This was how it felt going into battle.

Chapter Twenty Two

The king's feast

Tables had been set up along the full length of King Eormenric's hall, down either side and across the end, in the shape of a horse-shoe. And the doors had been left open to let in the cool evening air.

Fires burned and the late summer feast was under way.

More than two hundred men and women sat along the benches, or on the floor, or stood leaning against the walls, while the king and his most trusted warriors looked on from the high table.

There was meat and drink enough for everyone.

Soon the food would be cleared away and the women would leave. Then the drink would flow and the night would grow wild.

Soon, but not yet.

First Eormenric had a decision to make. He sat smiling and nodding as the feast went on, pretending to listen, but really thinking.

He knew about King Bricgnytt's great bridge at Robrivis. His men had reported back, watching as its timbers had been repaired.

And he knew about the Saxon raids on his land – three farms attacked this week alone. Jutrad had told him everything.

And Jutrad had prepared his warriors, ready for his order; ready for much greater numbers to be called up from the fields.

"Attack the bridge and take it now," Jutrad had urged. "Then *we* will be in control, not Bricgnytt. We will raid his lands, he will not raid ours."

It was a bold plan, and it seemed to make sense. But Eormenric had to decide.

He was King, not Jutrad, and he had the most to lose if things went badly.

He looked along the table at his son.

Aethelberht was still a young man coming into his full strength, laughing and horsing around with his friends. One day he would rule well.

But not if we are beaten in war.

If Eormenric made the wrong choice now he could lose his kingdom, and his son's kingdom, and the kingdom of all his sons to come…

"More wine, lord?"

"Of course."

The wine was good, fresh from Francia, and normally he would drink his fill. But not today. He raised the cup to his lips but sipped only lightly.

Maybe not a full war. Maybe a quick raid? Or something else to teach Bricgnytt a lesson?

Yes. Suddenly he put down his cup, and raised his hands for silence.

"Jutrad!" he called.

"Yes Lord?"

The warrior was seated close by, just along the table.

"Bring them in now," said Eormenric. "Bring in your Saxons."

****

A keen hush fell across the hall – and then a riot of jeering and laughing as the three prisoners were pushed in through the door.

They had been stripped of their weapons and even their boots. Their hands had been bound behind their backs with leather cords.

"Kneel before the king!" shouted someone.

And a chorus joined in.

"Kneel! Kneel!"

The young warriors were forced to their knees. A bone was tossed and it struck one – the dark haired one – hard on the face. The blow made his eyes sting and he looked up blinking back tears.

"They'll pay for this," growled Edwyn.

"It's fine… I'm not hurt…" whispered Kenhelm.

There was more laughter until Eormenric finally held up his hands for silence. He waited, stock still, and when he spoke his voice was strangely calm.

"Saxons," he said. "You came to my land to kill and to steal. No man does this without being punished. No man *or* woman."

He pointed at Sigwyn.

"Tell me. Does Bricgnytt send girls to raid for him now? Is he that desperate?"

The Jutes began laughing again.

"I am no raider!" called out Sigwyn. "I am a king's warrior! I came to your land with a message from my lord. We did not attack your farms – but your men set on us…"

She was shouting but her voice was lost under a torrent of jeers.

"You are here to listen girl," someone mocked. "Not to talk."

"Well *I'm* here to damned-well talk," another voice bellowed. And a great warrior shoved his way into the hall before anyone could stop him.

"Silence you fools!" he roared. "Bite your flapping tongues and hear me!"

The stranger's great frame seemed to fill the hall and he was shaking with rage. A shocked hush fell as he walked the length of the table and drew his sword. He glared around for a moment and then looked at King Eormenric.

"I don't suppose you remember me, cousin?" he said, calmly. "You were a small boy the last time I let you hold this sword. You held it well though, a fine lad you were – I told your father, you looked like a little Hengist."

"It… it can't be…Dragon-Flame? Beogard?"

"Aye," nodded Beogard. "Dragon-Flame. And she's as sharp as ever. Here – "

He tossed the weapon, handle first, to the king. Eormenric caught it lightly and stood, gazing in wonder at the blade.

In that moment of stillness, the man beside him – Jutrad – jumped up and drew a knife from his belt.

"I took that weapon from you," he growled at Beogard. "And now you dare bring it here? To this hall? It is death to raise a sword in front of the king!"

Beogard laughed.

"Enough yapping. You tried to steal that sword but you failed. A word of advice lad: next time you kill me make sure I'm actually dead."

Somebody sniggered.

Jutrad blushed and roared in fury at the insult. He clambered across the table and lunged with his knife – but Beogard side-stepped the blade.

Jutrad staggered past – but in the same movement he shot his arm backwards, almost too fast to see. His knife sliced across Beogard's mail shirt and cut into his beard. The old man staggered and Jutrad spun and levelled the blade to strike again, this time at his throat.

"Back off lad," growled Beogard. "Last chance. You'll get no more warnings from me…"

But Jutrad ignored him and thrust the knife at his face. Beogard ducked backwards and in one sudden movement grabbed his wrist, twisted it and sent him sprawling with a howl of pain.

Jutrad was up again in a heartbeat – but then a furious shout from Eormenric made him hesitate.

"Sit Jutrad! Sit man! Or I'll have you cut down. This warrior is my uncle!"

Jutrad stood uncertain, glaring still.

"But Lord! This is…"

"I said *sit*!"

Jutrad lowered his knife, still shaking with anger.

"Thank you king," called Beogard. "I see you are feasting but my business is urgent. Can we step outside and talk? Just for a moment?"

"If you wish. Yes."

Eormenric vaulted across the table. He passed Dragon-Flame back to Beogard.

"I thought you were long dead..."

"An easy mistake. Many have wished it..."

And they laughed.

"All of you, keep feasting!" Eormenric ordered, pointing at his men. "And see that no harm comes to these Saxons."

Beogard paused at the door, where Harnost and his kinsmen were waiting with Bron.

"King Eormenric – this young Jute warrior is Bron," said Beogard. "He has shown great courage. Can he untie the Saxons? They are his friends."

"Yes, do it," said Eormenric. "And let them eat."

*****

Bron ran forwards and used his knife to cut through the ropes.

"The slave boy?" grunted Kenhelm, rubbing

his wrists. "How did you come here? I'm glad to see you though."

"Never gladder," grinned Edwyn. "But you could have come quicker."

Sigwyn looked at Bron more closely, seeing his braided hair, and the amulet around his neck.

"He'll tell us his story soon enough," she said. "And look again friends. He's not a slave. He's a warrior."

****

Outside, Eormenric talked long into the evening with Beogard.

While the feasting grew loud in the hall they stood under the covered porch, where the warriors' spears and shields were stacked.

And at last King Eormenric clasped Beogard's shoulder.

"My thanks," he said. "You've given me much to think on."

Beogard smiled. "Good. A leader of men needs to think even more than he needs to fight."

They went back inside and found that the

torches were burning brightly and the singing was now full-hearted and loud. King Eormenric found the three East-Saxons sitting with their friend, the skinny Jute warrior, and he embraced each of them in turn.

"You will have gifts of friendship," he said. "For each of you risked your lives to reach my hall."

And Bron could never remember feeling as happy as he did that night.

The Saxons made him sit with them on the bench, and they made a great fuss of him joking and laughing about his warrior's gear.

"The hair-braiding isn't bad for a first attempt," said Kenhelm. "But we'll do it better for you tomorrow."

"Only if you can sit still," said Sigwyn. "And you'll need some new boots. And a decent tunic – that one stinks."

Edwyn nodded.

"Too right. We can't have our new Jute brother looking scruffy."

And while they spoke King Eormenric

crossed the hall with Beogard and they found Harnost, sitting with his kinsmen. The king embraced him.

"Your brother was killed wrongly," he said. "Jutrad is a brave warrior but he will pay for the killing, with blood or with treasure. Tomorrow he stands trial and you will have justice."

Harnost bowed and thanked the king. The law of the kingdom would be followed.

*****

"Where will you go after this?" asked Kenhelm.

He was standing with Bron outside the hall, watching as three drunken warriors staggered into the night. One of them tripped on something and the others stood over him laughing. Behind them, in the hall someone was attempting another song.

Bron shrugged.

"I...I haven't thought about it..."

"Back to your village?"

"No, the lad's coming with us of course."

It was Beogard. He appeared in the doorway,

his hair even more wild than usual and a drinking horn was slung about his neck on a golden chain.

He leaned against the door post and tried to straighten out his beard.

"Lost a bit of it in that fight…wonder if it'll grow back?…"

Then he looked at Bron.

"We have lots to do…much to see… you can come with me if you want to lad. But like I said, it's your choice. You have no debt to pay, not to me…"

"I do want to come," replied Bron at once. "I want nothing more."

"Good," nodded Beogard. "That's very good…it can be dangerous on the road, I need some protection…"

Then he belched, slid down the door post and slumped onto the floor.

"…now you lads should get some rest… I reckon you've both had too much beer… too much…"

And with that his head nodded and he began to snore.

Chapter Twenty Three

First lesson for a warrior

The days that followed were the most magical that Bron had ever spent in his life.

Early the next morning, even as the fire in the great hall still smouldered, King Eormenric's son Aethelberht gathered a group of friends together.

They were going to hunt deer in the lands to the south. And they asked Kenhelm to go with them.

"You like hunting?" the king's son asked the Saxon.

"Of course he does," said Edwyn. "He'll go with you if you lend him a good horse."

"Any will do me," Kenhelm grinned. "So long as it's fast."

So one was found and the hunting party raced out through the stronghold gates with Aethelberht at the front.

King Eormenric stood by his hall and watched them go.

And then he disappeared inside with his chief men and the doors were barred. Beogard went with them.

Edwyn and Sigwyn looked on, with Bron.

"They go to sit in judgement on Jutrad," said Edwyn grimly.

"I'm glad," said Sigwyn. "May the gods judge him too."

Then she turned to Bron.

"So now we have time to teach you how to fight, Jute brother."

*****

Of course Bron had held a sword before – Frumold's rusty old blade – but this was the first time somebody had showed him how to hold one properly, with a true grip.

The sun was shining down and Sigwyn took him to stand in a wide space beside the hall. He would never forget that first lesson.

Sigwyn gave him a practice blade, made of ash, and showed him how to stand.

"I'll hit at you. You block like this," she swung the sword smoothly and he copied her moves.

"Take care Bron," she said. "It may only be wood but when you get hit it will still hurt."

He nodded, determined to concentrate on what she told him.

After a few minutes he was already out of breath. And then she tripped him.

He sprawled on the ground, just as he had done the first day they met.

But this time Sigwyn reached out and straight away pulled him up again.

"I'm sorry," she said.

"It's fine," said Bron, blushing.

But Sigwyn put her arm around his shoulder.

"Enough practice for now," she said. "We'll find somewhere more quiet. Without an audience."

And then Bron noticed that they were being watched. A huddle of men stood beside the great hall, arms folded. One of them spat and looked away.

"They're friends of Jutrad," said Edwyn under his breath. "Be wary of them."

Bron felt his stomach tighten. The sooner he learnt to use a sword properly, the better.

"Don't worry," said Sigwyn calmly. "We are guests of the king."

And whether Jutrad's men meant to cause trouble they never found out. Because a moment later the hall doors were flung open and Beogard emerged.

It was almost as if the old warrior had known what everyone was thinking. He wiped his nose on his sleeve and walked straight over to Jutrad's men.

There he stood, with his fists on his belt and his feet apart, and spoke with them.

Bron was too far away to hear what was said, but after a minute Beogard threw back his head and laughed.

Then he clapped the nearest man on the shoulder. And suddenly they were all laughing.

King Eormenric came out now, followed by his chief men. Jutrad walked at the back, head bowed.

His life had been spared, Bron learnt later. But he would have to make a heavy payment in gold to Fornost's kin.

"King Eormenric is merciful," said Edwyn.

"Nay lad," answered Beogard. "He's clever. He still has a kingdom to defend and he needs fighters. Jutrad is more useful to him alive than dead."

*****

Two weeks passed. Bron became much better with his sword. The Saxons took turns at teaching him and almost without realising it he began to relax and to fight without thinking. When blows came, he blocked them, and when he hit back he moved more smoothly.

One afternoon, as he practised with Kenhelm beside the great hall, he became aware that he was being watched. King Eormenric and Beogard were standing nearby.

Bron focused on the fight.

Kenhelm lunged with his shield, then feigned a blow to his head – and at the same time swept a foot to trip him.

But this time Bron stepped back and kept his balance.

Sigwyn laughed.

"My warrior is too quick for you now!"

King Eormenric grunted his approval.

*****

The weather changed and the days grew cooler and wetter. Finally, at the start of the fourth week King Eormenric called Beogard and the Saxons to his hall again.

"The harvest is gathered and all is well. Tonight we feast," he said. "Then tomorrow we will leave here. You Saxons will ride ahead. Tell your king that I am ready to meet him at Robrivis."

The young warriors bowed.

"We will take your message lord," said Kenhelm. "And we'll tell our king how you welcomed us in your great hall."

Eormenric nodded.

"Good," he said. "But the bridge that he is building still troubles me. Lord Beogard tells me I am wrong. He says this wooden road can join our people in friendship. What do you think?"

"Lord Beogard is right. I'm sure of it," said Kenhelm.

"We will see," replied Eormenric. "I will meet King Bricgnytt at Robrivis and hear what he has to say. We Jutes do not fear war but neither do we seek it."

He stood and held out his arms to them.

"But that is for tomorrow. Tonight we feast — and I will have gifts for you all."

*****

Beogard, the Saxons and Bron piled out of the hall together and stood laughing in the autumn light. Edwyn put his arms around his friends.

"Our quest is successful. We've persuaded two kings to meet!"

"Yes. And I'm ready to travel again," said Sigwyn. "Now that I've seen the land of Jutes I want to go even further – maybe to the north, to Mercia? Or we could go west to the Weald to see your lands Lord Beogard?"

The others nodded.

"Wait up, not so fast lass," laughed Beogard. "We did well here. But it's not over yet. Not quite."

Epilogue

On a blustery autumn day, the morning after the harvest feast, a line of horses rode out from Cantwareburh.

King Eormenric left the stronghold with his chief warriors and they passed beneath the old Roman walls, and onto the road. The first leaves were starting to fall, and to bury the cobblestones as they did at this time each year.

Three young Saxons rode ahead on fine horses – gifts from the king – and a large man plodded along at the back, uncomfortable on a stout pony.

Beside him rode a young Jute warrior, straight-backed on a horse of his own.

The young warrior wore a new blue cloak in the fashion of the Jutes, but fastened at his shoulder with a Saxon-style brooch.

****

The king's party stopped twice on the journey. Once in Fefresham, where Eormenric and his son went to speak to a Frankish smith. And while they talked – about weapons, and gold and the latest news from Francia – the smith's sister slipped away.

She went to find the old warrior, and the young Jute, and they spoke quietly together about business of their own.

She gave them gifts, wrapped in a bundle of cloth.

The second time the riders stopped was a short way beyond the town, in a place beside the road. Here a grave was marked with a pile of stones. They stayed for a moment, while the wind tugged at their cloaks and a light rain touched their faces.

The old warrior stood with his head bowed and offered up a prayer to Thunor, the god of thunder; Thunor his own the god, the god of courage.

****

Finally, they travelled on to Robrivis on the far western border of the kingdom. And they waited in the mud beside the river, where a great bridge of oak timbers stretched across to the other side.

Soon another party arrived. A group of East-Saxon warriors came across the bridge.

And King Eormenric and King Bricgnytt met, and finally exchanged their vows of peace.

"Now let this bridge be a link between you and not a cause for war," said Beogard. "And if enemies attack either of your kingdoms – be they raiders from the river or armies from overland – you will cross it and come to each other's aid."

And saying this, he beckoned forward the young Jute, holding the bundle of cloth.

And he unwrapped it.

"These are yours," he said. "Keep them as a

sign of friendship between your kingdoms. I'll be watching."

And he gave each king a sword, finely made.

Each had a dragon-flame blade and a ring on the handle like the sword of Hengist.

Appendix

Fact *vs* Fiction

The real story of the Anglo-Saxons

N.S.Blackman

Fact vs Fiction

Names of characters in Freedom for Bron

Some of the names in this story are taken from real historical figures. **Eormenric** and **Aethelberht** were kings in eastern Kent during the later AD 500s.

It was common for Anglo-Saxon names to be created by joining two words together.
For example the name Aethelberht came from 'aethel' (noble) and 'beorht' (bright).
The name **Kenhelm** (or Cenelm) is from 'cene' (keen/bold) and 'helm' (helmet).
Many Anglo-Saxon names follow this pattern.

About the Anglo-Saxons

But for the purposes of my story I needed to make some names up.

Where I have done this my main aim was to make them sound good to modern ears.

For example the character name **Beogard** came loosely from beorg (meaning hill) and geard (meaning enclosure) – the two added together suggest strength and size, both well suited to the character.

Bron is based on the word 'brun' which simply means brown or black.

Other names are completely made up simply because I like the sound of them, not because they are based on any real words.

The name **Paega** is not based on anything but it seemed to suit the man.

There are several other examples in the story,

Fact vs Fiction

such as **Fornost** and his brother **Harnost**. It should be remembered that the dialect spoken by the Jutes would have included words and names that we don't know about because they were never written down.

I had fun with **King Bricgnytt**: the Anglo-Saxon word 'bricg' translates as bridge and 'nytt' means use, so there's a clue in his name.

About the Anglo-Saxons

Freedom for Bron
some questions answered

Why does Beogard like drinking ale so much?

A warrior like Beogard would have loved feasting but that's not the only reason he talks about beer so much – ale was a part of everyday life for most people.

It was probably a less alcoholic drink than modern beer though and it had the important

Fact vs Fiction

advantage of not carrying diseases or parasites. There was no water purification in Anglo-Saxon times so every time you drank water you risked getting ill.

Were there really female warriors like Sigwyn in Anglo-Saxons times?

It would have been unusual – and in the story Bron is surprised when he's knocked down by Sigwyn. But women, like men, commonly carried a type of knife (called a seax) which could have been used as a tool or a weapon. In the dangerous 5th and 6th centuries women may well have

About the Anglo-Saxons

expected to defend themselves and their homes – but that's not quite the same thing as being a full warrior. However, there are some examples of weapons being found in graves with female bones, leading some historians to believe that women sometimes were warriors.

One historical example, from the 10th century, is King Alfred's daughter Aethelfled, who was a commander in wars against the Danes.

Whether she personally fought in battle is not known but it's certainly possible. She was a renowned war leader and earned the name 'Lady of the Mercians'.

Fact vs Fiction

Was there really a 'sword of Hengist' called Dragon-Flame?

According to legend Hengist was the Germanic leader who was the first Saxon to conquer territory in Britain. In the stories he arrives with his brother Horsa and three ships full of warriors in the east of Kent.

At first Hengist and Horsa are paid by the Britons to fight against Picts from the north. But then they turn against their paymasters and take land for themselves.

We can't be sure whether this legendary Hengist is based on a real historical figure or not, but later Anglo-Saxon writers seemed to believe so.

Some of the Anglo-Saxon royal families claimed to be descended from Hengist (just as Beogard does in the story).

About the Anglo-Saxons

The sword Dragon-Flame was made up for this story but the most valued swords of the period really did have 'pattern welded' blades and famous swords were given names and passed on as heirlooms.

Archaeologists have also found a particular style of 'ring sword' from this period which has a decorative ring fixed to the hilt.

The ring's purpose is unclear but it may have been a special sign that the sword was a gift from a king, or connected to some promise or oath of loyalty.

Fact vs Fiction

Was Bricgnytt a real king?

No. There *was* probably a king in west Kent at the time and one of his strongholds was Robrivis (modern Rochester). But if he existed his name is not recorded.

However a king called Eormenric is recorded as ruling the Jute lands of eastern Kent, with a stronghold at Canterbury.

And Eormenric's son Aethelberht – the one who takes Kenhelm hunting in the story – is an important figure in later Anglo-Saxon history. He was the first king to adopt Christianity and he introduced the first written laws in Anglo-Saxon England.

About the Anglo-Saxons

Are Cloda and Cleava real figures?

Whilst these two characters are entirely fictional there do seem to have been some highly skilled craftspeople working in gold, glass and precious materials in Kent at this time. And there is evidence for close links with Francia (modern France). It's quite possible that Frankish smiths settled in Kent and made fine jewellery and weapons for the rich and powerful.

Fact vs Fiction

What was the medicine that Cleava gave to Beogard?

Anglo-Saxons didn't have any of the modern medicine that we take for granted so people had to use traditional herbal remedies, charms and practises such as blood-letting.

It's now recognised that the mind can have a powerful effect on the body, so perhaps some of these charms would have worked if the sick person really believed in them – although that wouldn't have helped much against the many serious illnesses that were prevalent, and that made life-expectancy so low. At the very least charms would have provided some comfort.

In the story, when Beogard lies dying, it is because he has lost all hope. Perhaps getting his sword back is as much a cure as Cleava's potion.

About the Anglo-Saxons

Beside the fire Beogard tells a tale about a supernatural dog - were Anglo-Saxon warriors really interested in stories like that?

Yes – Anglo-Saxons loved story telling and they were definitely interested in supernatural creatures as well as the wild animals from the world around them such as wolves, bears and boars. Many such creatures decorate their jewellery and armour. And we have even more important evidence of their interest in fantastic creatures, recorded in the Old English poem Beowulf – an epic story of warriors fighting monsters and demons.

Fact vs Fiction

Do we really know how Anglo-Saxon warriors spoke and acted?

We can only tell so much by studying Anglo-Saxon bones and fragments of treasure. Imagine if we could actually sit beside a fire, as Bron did, and listen to a real warrior's tale.

Well in a way we can.

Early Anglo-Saxons didn't write things down but by a lucky chance one of their great stories did survive: *Beowulf*.

This exciting tale was probably told and re-told many times over the years before it was

About the Anglo-Saxons

finally written down by Christian monks who *could* read and write.

The story of Beowulf is told in an Old English dialect and when we read it we can hear a tale much as Anglo-Saxons may have heard it in their feasting halls.

In this epic, a hero warrior called Beowulf helps a king by battling against a monster, a demon and a dragon.

The poem gives us important clues about how Anglo-Saxon warriors talked, dressed, armed themselves and behaved.

Note: this unique story nearly didn't make it into modern times. Having survived for around a thousand years as the only written copy it was almost destroyed in a fire in 1731 – the marks from the fire can still be seen around the edges of the manuscript today. It was a lucky escape.

Fact vs Fiction

Was there really a bridge at Robrivis?

Yes, centuries earlier the Romans had built a wooden bridge across the river. But we don't know how much of it was still standing by Anglo-Saxon times. Unlike the Romans the Anglo-Saxons were not known for being great engineers. They must have been skilled at working with wood because they built ships and great feasting halls, all without the help of modern tools. But compared with the Romans before them, and the Normans who came after,

About the Anglo-Saxons

they weren't very ambitious builders

Was Cantware a real place?

Yes, the setting for the story is north Kent – and today if you stand with your back to the fields and look out across the estuary you realise what a tempting place this must have been for sea-raiders to attack. There are sheltered inlets and

Fact vs Fiction

creeks where boats could be moored unseen. And there are islands where you could set up camp ready to plunder the land beyond.

In the story *Freedom for Bron* Beogard warns the farmers to keep a close watch on the river. That would have been good advice.

With no professional army to deter raiders ordinary people had to be watchful and ready to defend themselves.

About the Anglo-Saxons

Who were the Jutes and Saxons? And did the really fight each other?

The people living in southern Britain in the 6th century were probably a mixture of the original Romano-British and groups of new Germanic settlers (see map).

The Germanic tribes (the Angles, Saxons and Jutes) eventually came to be called Anglo-Saxons – and later still, they called themselves English.

In *Freedom for Bron* the Jutes and the

Arrival of Germanic tribes in the 5th century

Fact vs Fiction

Saxons view each other with suspicion – and that may have been the case in real life too.

For although the two groups probably spoke a similar language and followed similar gods, they had their own separate customs.

For example the Jutes had their own styles of jewellery and clothing. They had their own way of burying their dead too, as we know from graves that have been found.

About the Anglo-Saxons

What religion did Anglo-Saxons believe in?

Strange figures of gods stare out at us from gold ornaments, locked behind glass in museum cabinets: mysterious horned beings with spears, dragons and fantastic creatures whose names we can only guess at.

These are all that remain of Anglo-Saxon traditional religion – beliefs dismissed as 'pagan' by later Christian writers. What the early Anglo-Saxons believed we can't be sure because

Fact vs Fiction

they didn't have holy books or write their ideas down.

But perhaps this sense of mystery and strangeness is not out of place. Maybe it would have been felt by young Anglo-Saxons too as they looked at images of the gods, or visited shrines.

For them religion would not have been about reading sacred texts but about listening to stories at the fireside on stormy nights, hearing whispered superstitions, trying not to offend ghosts and spirits, and copying rituals picked up from elders.

Life was hard and death was an everyday reality. It's little wonder that people believed in the power of the supernatural, to help them or harm them.

About the Anglo-Saxons

There was no science to explain why things happened. What made crops grow? Why did people get sick? How could you bring yourself good luck, or cure a toothache?

For early Anglo-Saxons the answers could only lie with the gods – and when rain ruined your crops or your livestock fell sick, you could only hope that some supernatural power might save you. People believed that deities and magical

Left: special places in the landscape - including notable trees, hills or pools - may have been used as shrines where offerings would be left to the gods.
In the story Bron approaches the 'moss-covered stone' in its sacred grove - and his hair prickles as he feels the gods watching him.

Fact vs Fiction

creatures inhabited the landscape around them – dwarfs, elfs, demons, dragons.

And long after Woden, Thunor and Frigg were forgotten as gods their names lingered on in the days of our week – Wednesday, Thursday and Friday – and maybe as well in place names such as Woodnesborough (Kent) and Thundersley (Essex).

The goddess Eostra, whose feast was once celebrated in April, is remembered in our word Easter.

The lives of the early Anglo-Saxons may now be hidden in the mists of time but with a little imagination we can still feel their presence - especially in the landscapes where they lived.